GODSHOME

ROBERT SHECKLEY

A TOM DOHERTY ASSOCIATES BOOK
NEW YORK

This is a work of fiction. All the characters and events portrayed in this novel are either fictitious or are used fictitiously.

GODSHOME

This book is printed on acid-free paper.

Book design by Scott Levine

Edited by David G. Hartwell

A Tor Book
Published by Tom Doherty Associates, LLC
175 Fifth Avenue
New York, NY 10010

www.tor.com

Tor® is a registered trademark of Tom Doherty Associates, LLC.

Library of Congress Cataloging-in-Publication Data

Sheckley, Robert.
Godshome / Robert Sheckley.
    p.   cm.
"A Tor book"—T.p. verso.
ISBN 0-312-86804-9 (hc)
ISBN 0-312-86803-0 (pbk)
I. Title.
PS3569.H392 G63 1999
813'.54—ddc21   98-31618
                                                     CIP

First Hardcover Edition: January 1999
First Trade Paperback Edition: January 2000

Printed in the United States of America

0   9   8   7   6   5   4   3   2   1

To Gail, my wife, my love, my destiny.

GODSHOME

PROLOGUE

IN A REGION THAT LAY AT RIGHT ANGLES TO, BUT SEPARATE from, the usual spacetime, all was as quiet as it had been for a near eternity. Everything about this region was in a state of potentiality. There was no land, no air, no water, no atoms or quarks, no electrons, no photons, not even any neutrinos, those infinitesimal wanderers of the spaces.

Here there was no light and no darkness, because both photons and antiphotons existed only in a state of potentiality so close to nonbeing as to be a purely negligible quantity. The becoming of this potentiality could not be said to exist yet, but it might have existed yesterday and it could exist tomorrow.

Into this place, a signal came winging. Upon penetrating the space, potentiality gave up its long sleep, not without a certain reluctance, and flip-flopped into actuality.

An atmosphere formed up for the signal to resound in. Photons appeared so that the signal might become visible. Intelligent, godlike beings formed so that the signal could be heard and understood.

First there was nothing at all, and then there was a meadow sparkling with dew. Each dewdrop glistened with an individual luster. One of the dewdrops began to expand.

Color flashed on its transparent spherical sides. It continued to grow until it burst. From this stepped a human-shaped being. This being waited and watched while other drops of dew expanded, swelled, and popped, revealing other gods. At last twelve places were filled. The High Gods, ancient as the universe, new as the morning, stood upon the grass and contemplated one another. They knew what they had been born to do. They awaited the birth of the one who would put that plan into action. The one called Asturas.

PART 1

CHAPTER 1

EVERY OCCUPATION HAS ITS FANS. IF YOU'RE A ROCK STAR, there are people ready to throw themselves at your feet and swear allegiance to your lips and eyes and hair. But if you're Arthur Fenn, a Ph.D. in comparative mythology with several publications to your credit, your fan may be no more than an old foreign gentleman with a short white beard and a brown seamed face. Still, it takes only a single fan to bring about change in your life.

Arthur was in his early thirties, somewhat on the tall side, with a scholar's stoop. He was presently unemployed: few universities needed a mythologist with Arthur's meager credentials. He owned a cottage, left to him by his parents, and a bare income from their insurance. He had a fiancée, the beautiful Mimi, though the relationship was going through one of its rockier phases at the moment.

But a fan? Arthur hadn't known he had one until the day Mr. Avodar came by his Florida cottage. It was a typically sultry day in Tahiti Beach, Florida, capital of Magnolia County to the west of Dade and Broward Counties. The county had been carved out of reclaimed land after the Florida Swamplands Reclamation program dried up half the Everglades, decimating the alligators and snowy egrets and provided new land for Florida's ever-growing population of retirees and fruit pickers. Tahiti Beach was a nondescript little city with a population 300,000, most of them recent immigrants from the tumultuous regions of Central America.

It was a hot day, as usual. Even the cypress planking that made up Arthur's cottage was sweating, as were the joists and ties and various other bits of lumber that held the place together. Arthur was only half sweating. The front half of him was facing the air conditioner, which blew cool air on his chest. His back, however, knew no such relief, and so it sweated without cease. Arthur was seated at his old oak roll-top desk, inherited from his father, trying to make sense of his income tax.

There came a knock at the door. Arthur stood up, glad of any relief, slipped on a short-sleeve shirt, and went to answer it.

An old man with a short white beard and a brown seamed face stood there.

"Dr. Fenn," the old man said, with an accent that might have been formed in the Murmad section of Damascus, probably close to the Aleppo gate, to judge by the truncated sibilants. "I am so happy to meet you. You look much better than your photograph."

"Where did you see my photograph?" Arthur asked.

"In the *Journal of Canaanite Antiquities*. They ran it in the issue containing your remarkable article."

"Which article was that?"

"It was entitled 'The Key to Conversation with the Gods: A Pre-Islamic Ritual as Revealed in Modern-day Ashwari Practice.' I am Mr. Avodar, by the way."

Arthur remembered that he'd paid fifty dollars for the honor of being included in the journal, but they hadn't charged him anything extra for running his picture and a short bio.

"Well, come in, Mr. Avodar," Arthur said. He cleared magazines and newspapers from the couch, urged his visitor to sit, and asked if he could bring him coffee or tea.

"Nothing at all," the old man said. "I am on my way to relatives in Hialeah. I have a taxi waiting outside. I just wanted to take this opportunity to meet you and express my very great pleasure at your article."

The article had described an ancient Canaanite text which Arthur had found mentioned in a seventeenth-century French account of explorations in greater Syria by a M. Dubrocq.

Dubrocq's article had never been translated into English. It contained an account Dubrocq claimed to have heard firsthand from his dragoman, Ali, concerning the ancient and infamous key to "conversation with the gods." Ali claimed this was the very key that King Solomon had used to call up demons, dieties, and spirits. According to Dubrocq, it was the lost key that magicians, seers, and alchemists had sought ever since. A copy of the key was said to have been owned by Nicholas Flamel, received from the hand of a man known as Abraham the Jew, this in the late 1300s. Flamel's Tower still stands in Paris, on the right bank, not far from Chatelet, but the key has been missing for many years.

"Yes, I wrote the article," Arthur said. "I presented it as an interesting legend, no more."

"I am aware of that," Mr. Avodar said. "I wish to add some information to your account."

Arthur offered his guest a seat. Avodar took up his story.

His family, he told Arthur, had for many centuries been custodians of Solomon's key, entrusted with it by the Wijis, the original holders, who had gotten it from Solomon himself.

This family had died out, the last member falling at the battle of Lepanto.

"And so it came to us, the Avodars," Mr. Avodar said. "And
we held it as a sacred trust for all these years."

He unwrapped the package. Inside, covered in many lay-
ers of oiled silk, was an ancient book written in Hebrew, with
wooden covers fastened with rivets of copper.

Arthur held the book reverently. "Thank you for showing
this to me."

"Oh, I intend more than that," Avodar said. "Take it, my
dear Dr. Fenn. It is yours. I present it to you."

"I could not possibly accept it," Arthur said. "It must be
beyond price."

"It is priceless indeed," Avodar said. "Yet, paradoxically, it
is of no value to me. Or rather, it has a great negative value,
since my possession of it could cost me my life."

"I don't understand," Arthur said.

"Objects such as this," Avodar said, "are outlawed in
present-day Syria, where they are considered pagan blasphemy of the worst kind."

"Surely they must understand that you don't worship it?
That it's an object of antiquarian interest?"

"The atmosphere in present-day Syria is such that objects
of far less significance than this have cost men their lives. Fa-
naticism thrives when uncovering apostasy, even when none
exists. I should have destroyed this long ago. But by the time
I fully understood my danger, it was too late. I managed to escape from my country and come to America. Here I will begin
a new life."

"Why don't you sell the book?" Arthur asked. "It would be
worth plenty to an antiquarian book dealer."

"Its intrinsic value, without a provenance which I cannot
supply, would probably be no more than a few hundred dollars. I prefer to give it to you, Dr. Fenn. I hope it brings you
better luck than it did me."

Put like that, Arthur could do no more than accept. Mr.
Avodar left shortly after that, riding off in his taxi to join his
family in Hialeah. Arthur put the wooden-covered book away
and didn't think about it until after his experience with
Sammy.

CHAPTER 2

GETTING SOLOMON'S KEY WAS A BIT OF GOOD LUCK. LATER that week Arthur had another bit of good luck, or what seemed like it at the time. He received a letter from a lawyer in Miami informing him that his Uncle Seymour, he of the dour mouth and droll eye, had written Arthur into his will, perhaps on a whim, since the two hadn't talked in years, and had done this just two days before choking to death on a stone crab in Joe's Stone Crab in Miami Beach. Enclosed was a check for twenty-two thousand dollars.

Arthur immediately telephoned his best friend, Sammy Gluck.

"Twenty-two thousand is a nice little sum," Sammy told him when they met that evening at Thank God It's Friday on the old A1A highway that passed through Tahiti Beach.

"But it's not a useful sum," Sammy added.

"My feelings exactly," Arthur said. "It was good of Uncle Seymour, of course. I never even thought he liked me. But frankly, I wish he'd left me a lot more or a lot less. It's not enough to start a business with and it's too much to waste at the dog track."

"It is just the right sum," Sammy said. Sammy was a skinny young man in his early twenties with wiry black hair and a deep tennis tan. He wore a crisp Madras sport shirt, fawn-colored slacks, and tasseled white loafers.

"How do you figure?"

"It is just the right sum," Sammy said, "to invest in a high-risk proposition that could multiply your money tenfold or leave you without any. Especially when the odds greatly favor the former outcome."

"The tenfold one?" Arthur asked, just to make sure he was registering this correctly.

"That's the one I mean," Sammy said. "In the unlikely event you get wiped out, you could just forget you ever got Uncle Seymour's bequest. But if this little deal pays off, you're set up with some really useful money. I have ideas for that, too."

Sammy was a junior broker in Collins, Aimtree & Dissendorf, a stock brokerage house in a one-story blue stucco building on Tahiti Beach's Miracle Mile, just past the Winn-Dixie and before you got to the Wal-Mart.

Many thoughts might have gone through Arthur's mind at that moment. It was his misfortune that he came up with those dangerous lines from Kipling's famous poem for losers called "If."

If you can make one heap of all your winnings
And risk it on one turn of pitch and toss,
And lose, and turn again to your beginnings,
And never breathe a word about your loss . . .

Stirring words, especially for a man like Arthur who thought his character needed some bracing.

"Tell me about the proposition," he said.

Sammy ordered another Harvey Wallbanger and told

Arthur about Amalgamated Mining of Bahia, a Brazilian gold mining stock being offered on the Vancouver stock exchange. His own firm had taken a modest position in the venture.

The only thing Arthur knew about Brazilian gold mining stocks was that they were sure to fail. This was hard-won wisdom handed down from father to son. Arthur mentioned this to Sammy.

"Exactly," Sammy said, with a grin.

"Exactly what?" Arthur asked.

"Amalgamated Mining of Bahia is sure to fail. Practically guaranteed. These fools are mining in a volcanic zone that was played out fifty years ago. Rumor is they've salted the mine—put enough gold into the ground to get up some interest. On the strength of that, they've made some big announcements. For some crazy reason, the stock is zooming."

"Thank you," Arthur said.

"I beg your pardon?"

"You've already succeeded in talking me out of it. Shall we go to jai lai this evening or the dog track?"

"No, no, you don't understand," Sammy said. "I don't want you to buy this stock in hope of it *appreciating*. I want you to buy it in the almost certain expectation that it is going to *fall through the floor* within the week."

"Why don't I just make paper airplanes out of my money and throw it to the wind?" Arthur suggested. "It would be a more amusing way of going broke than what you're outlining."

"You still don't get it," Sammy said. "I'm not advising you to buy the stock expecting it to *rise*. I'm advising you to take a short position, expecting it to *fall.*"

"I don't really understand these matters," Arthur said. "Sumerian and Hittite mythology is my field, not the stock market."

"I am trying to explain. When you sell short, you buy an option to sell stock at a certain price within a certain time. If the stock appreciates in value, you're out the money invested. If it falls, you make a killing. Especially since with twenty-two thousand dollars and my personal guarantee, I'll be able to leverage your holding. This will enable you to take an option on a much bigger piece of the stock than you'd normally be able to. Then, for every point the stock falls when your option falls due, you'll make . . . let me see . . . "

Sammy began writing rapidly on the paper tablecloth, scrawling figures with wild abandon. Arthur could feel the dollars expanding in his pocket already. The numbers were impressive. And he liked the idea of betting with smart money. It seemed to him the height of sophistication to bet that a worthless stock would go down.

Nevertheless, a final soupçon of caution caused him to pause. "And all I can lose is my stake?"

"That's just about the worst outcome," Sammy said. "And the least likely. What is much *more* likely is that you'll make a fortune and I'll be declared a genius and made a partner in the firm."

"Are you investing in this stuff yourself?"

Sammy nodded solemnly. "I'm selling it short with every cent I can beg, borrow, or borrow."

CHAPTER 3

"BUT HOW? HOW COULD IT HAVE FAILED?" ARTHUR ASKED, that dolorous morning four days later when Sammy telephoned with the bad news.

"It's the damndest break I've ever seen," Sammy said. "And I've been in this business for almost three years. The bottom was just about to fall out of Amalgamated of Bahia when all of a sudden a worthless test shaft the company had run just to satisfy the comptrollers went through a dome— that's a technical term in geology—"

"Get to it," Arthur said grimly.

"—and whammo, the bit came up like gold-plated. They'd hit some crazy mother lode—a solid vein that shouldn't have been there and makes the Kimberley look like a pile of shit."

Arthur was to remember that expression much later, when all this was history and he had problems so much bigger that he could almost look back on the days of his ruin as the good old days. But for now he was plenty steamed. "So I'm wiped out?"

"I'm afraid it's a little worse than that," Sammy said.

"How could it be worse than that? You lose a hundred percent and you're out of the game, right?"

"Not if you're in on leverage," Sammy said. "Look, I'm in the same position."

Somehow that wasn't the comfort Sammy might have expected it to be. Funny how your broker's loss is never your gain.

"What do you mean, I'm in on leverage?" Arthur asked.

"I explained it to you. You only had to put up a small percentage to buy your block of shares. If it had gone down, you'd have made a fortune, just like I told you. But since it's gone the way it has—well, I'm afraid you owe a fortune."

"How much of a fortune?" Arthur asked.

In a very low, almost whispery voice, Sammy said, "Just short of a million."

"Dollars?"

Sammy nodded. "As of this moment. The stock is climbing like a rocket."

"Climbing? You mean things could get worse?"

"They could," Sammy admitted. "But they also could get better. A whole lot better. That's why I've delayed selling you out."

"Aside from me dropping dead," Arthur said, "how could my position get better?"

"Amalgamated's find is located right next to a volcano. The damned thing could blow any time. If that happened, the gold would be lost under millions of metric tons of magma, the stock would plummet, and you'd be sitting pretty."

"How likely is that?" Arthur asked.

"With volcanoes, you can never tell."

"When was the last time this particular volcano blew?"

"August of 1867," Sammy said miserably.

"Sammy, sell me out."

"Arthur, it *could* blow!"

"No, I want out."

"Can you pay the mil?"

Arthur shook his head, then, remembering that Sammy

couldn't see him, said, "You know that twenty-two thousand was all the money I've got. Aside from a hundred and thirty bucks in my checking account."

"You're in trouble," Sammy said. "I hate to say this, but it's true. They're going to come after you for the money."

"I suppose that's logical," Arthur said, hearing his own voice echo in his ears as though his head were hollow. "What do you suggest I do?"

"You want it straight?"

"No, tie it up in pink ribbons. Of course I want it straight!"

"You'd better hold on to the stock," Sammy said. "If you get out now, you owe more than you can pay. If you hold on a few days longer, you'll owe more than that, but you'll at least have a chance at that volcano blowing."

"Yeah," Arthur said, the enormity of his position just beginning to sink in upon the trembling tabula rasa of his mind. "I guess I'll hold on . . . how long can I hold on?"

"You've got another three days," Sammy said. "Unless you can raise fifty thousand more and extend your option."

"I guess I'll take the three days," Arthur said. He couldn't think what to say after that. Finally he said, "This volcano. What's it called?"

"Ixtruehembla," Sammy said. "In some Brazilian Indian language that means 'Crazy Monkey.' "

"Thanks. I just wanted to know what they should write on my tombstone."

"Hey, come on, buddy! Maybe something'll turn up."

"And maybe they'll find a secret codicil to Uncle Seymour's will in which, on second thought, he decided to give me another five hundred thousand."

"Is that likely?" asked Sammy, ever hopeful.

"It's likelier than Ixtruehembla blowing up in time to save my ass."

Arthur hung up and reached for a cigarette. At least he was no longer afraid of dying of lung cancer. In fact, at the

moment it seemed an outcome more to be desired rather
than the likelier alternative, a stretch at Raiford prison for
whatever they called it when you bought stuff big-time with
money you didn't have.

He thought for a moment and it came to him. Grand lar-
ceny. That was what they called it.

CHAPTER 4

SO THERE HE WAS, ARTHUR, SITTING IN THE FLORIDA ROOM OF his quaint little bungalow in Tahiti Beach, Florida, with the air conditioner wheezing away and creating the illusion of coolness, enough to fool his mind, although his body still persisted in sweating profusely. There he was, a man who, in one inconsidered swoop, had converted an asset of twenty-two thousand dollars into a liability of close to a million and growing every day. And, being a purposeful animal, he asked himself, "What now?" His own inconsequential mind replied, "What indeed?"

No good thoughts came to him in that delirium of apprehension that signals the imminent arrival of a world of trouble. Could he raise the money he owed, or any significant portion of it? No way, José, as the local fruit pickers were wont to say. Could he run away, perhaps to the real Tahiti? That idea was about a hundred years out of date: they could extradite you from anywhere, and anyhow, what good had leaving it all behind done Gauguin?

Arthur's mind, overloaded with acuities of anguish, rebelled at considering so-called practical solutions, and turned instead to the one subject he knew something about: com-

parative mythology, a subject in which he was qualified to
teach, had there been a college or university in the United
States interested in hiring him. But it was not thoughts of
teaching that presently filled his overtaxed brain. He was
thinking now of Hasamdemeli, the Hittite god of blacksmiths,
said to concern himself with lost causes. He was thinking of
Haukim, one of the old south Arabian gods of wisdom, and of
Haubas, better known as Attar, another south Arabian diety,
believed to take on androgynous traits in his/her Akkadian
manifestation. How dear they all seemed to him now! And
how distant he would soon be from them, breaking rocks in
a Florida penitentiary while thousands jeered.

These old and forgotten gods were inexpressively dear to
him because Arthur didn't have a practical bone in his long,
bony body. In his heart of hearts he was a superstitious worshipper of ancient and forgotten dieties. That was why in college he had majored in superstition under the guise of
comparative mythology.

Ah, but where were they now, his lost gods? Out there in
the nothingness of time inconsidered. Mere figments of
mankind's predilection for mystery. Or so the scholars would
have you believe. But what made Haukim and Haubas any
less real than the God of the Christians, the Allah of the
Moslems, or the Buddha of the Buddhists? In what way were
St. Francis and St. Christopher any less real than Harum and
Haruna, those snake-shaped water spirits of ancient tribal Mo-
rocco? If St. Jude was believed by millions to be the saint of
lost causes, why not Hendursanga of the Sumerians, who cor-
responded to the Akkadian god Isum and was believed to be
connected with the proper functioning of a nation's laws, and
with justice in general?

For many, these dieties would be considered no more
than vile superstitions. But it all depended on who was doing
the name-calling. The victors get to call the shots, dietywise,

and to say what was deep and spiritual and true. But who was to say they were right in the great and mysterious scheme of things?

Nothing was left for Arthur now but prayer. But who was he to pray to? Not the regulation dieties of the standard religions, in whom he had never believed and who, even at this dolorous pass, he couldn't bring himself to turn to. Who should he address but the dieties, demons and devils he had studied and dreamed about from childhood on?

Feeling curiously lightheaded, Arthur got up from his chair and went to the garage, which he had converted into a storeroom and office, leaving his car to bake outside in the sun. Mellow light filled with dust motes filtered through the louvered window set high in the slanted ceiling. There was a smell of antiquity here, a comforting feeling of time out of mind.

Prayer was all that was left to him. So he would pray, but to the demons and dieties of his own choice.

Lifting a drop cloth, Arthur opened a drawer in his father's old desk. From it he took the little stone amulet he had bought one summer when he had gone on a guided tour of pre-Islamic ruins, given by the Syrian Department of Antiquities. It was a tan-colored stone carved in the shape of an eagle with a lion's head. He'd bought it in a stall in the bazaar at Aleppo. Undoubtedly a fake. But it was similar to what the ancient Akkadians had used for their thaumaturgical rites.

Clutching the little object, Arthur went to the nineteenth-century tomes put together by the English polymath William Dean Scott. He selected volume five, prayers and incantations to call up demons, devils, and familiars. Then, just for luck, he took out the book that his fan, Mr. Avodar, had given him, *The Key to Conversation with the Gods*.

Like one drunk on strong wine, he gathered the ingredients he would need for the ceremony: the candles, the dried lizard skin, the cup of sour milk, and the golden drops of honey. Pricking his finger with an imitation Sabaean dagger, he added a few drops of his blood to the mixture. And then, finding the right page in *The Key*, and translating the ancient Hebrew with difficulty, he intoned the ceremonial words, feeling lightheaded and giddy and devil-may-care.

Nothing happened.

Feeling completely out of his mind, he said the words again, this time with his best imitation of a Sumerian accent. Again, nothing.

Maybe a west Sumerian accent would do better? He tried that. Nothing.

"Shit," he said.

A voice from out of nowhere said, "What did you say?"

"I said 'shit,' " Arthur said.

"I don't believe you have the pronunciation quite right."

"Shite?" Arthur hazarded.

"That's it! You got it!"

There was a small clap of thunder and a miniscule flash of lightning, all within his garage, and then a twisting of smoke began to appear, spinning like a miniature blue tornado on the gray concrete garage floor. The tornado wobbled, took on green and red colors, and solidified into the shape of a small red structure. It took a moment for Arthur to recognize this as a scaled-down copy of an English telephone box, no more than three feet high, with a tiny telephone inside.

A thousand questions flooded Arthur's mind. He stared at the phone box with a hangdog gaze of dull amaze, aware that if he were to think logically about what was happening it would surely vanish like the baseless vision it undoubtedly was. This was no time for dumb questions like "Gee, how did that happen?" Dull-minded and prosy interrogations drove away the few miracles that the powers at large were pleased to grant. No, this was happening to him and he was determined to go along with the flow.

In a moment of pure insight, Arthur lifted the telephone and said into it, "Hello, is anyone there?"

A voice came back through the sound box. It said, "Kindly deposit five shekels for the first five minutes."

Arthur scrabbled wildly in his pockets, taking out six quarters, two dimes, and a host of pennies before realizing that these were unlikely to be accepted as substitutes for the ancient coin called a shekel. But where was he to find shekels? He had an image of himself flying to New York, breaking into the Museum of Natural History after midnight, and cannibalizing their collection of mid-Eastern coins. But he had neither the plane fare nor the time.

Maybe whoever was responsible for this apparition or whatever it was also converted currency? He stuffed all his quarters into the slot and waited.

The voice said, "You have deposited too much money. Sorry, we cannot make change."

"Never mind," Arthur said.

"To whom did you wish to speak?"

Arthur hadn't thought this far into the matter. He choked, gasped, and finally took the plunge. "Any demon who happens to be free."

"I am sorry, sir, the demons were retired from service quite some time ago."

"You mean you have no active demons?"

"The whole line has been withdrawn for restructuring. Is there anyone else you'd like to talk to?"

"Let me speak to a god, then."

"Yes, sir. Which god?"

"Which gods have you got?"

"The list would take several hours to recite. We are not an information service. If you do not know the name of the diety you wish to speak to, kindly clear the line for another user."

"Wait! I want to talk to Haukim!"

"He is not currently available."

"Hasdrubal?"

"His telephone number is unlisted."

"Attar?"

"Not currently available."

"Any god!"

"There is no diety named 'any god,' " the voice said severely. "You probably need an information service. Good-bye and have a nice—"

"Wait! Get me an information service!"

"Which one?"

"The most popular one!"

"There is no service called 'The Most Popular One.' "

"Give me the first one in the directory!" Arthur said in a flash of inspiration.

"You are quite sure of that?" the telephone voice asked.

"Entirely sure! Please! Please!"

"No need to grovel," the telephone voice said. "Not to me, at any rate. Just a moment and I will connect you."

Arthur waited, scarcely daring to hope. A plan had come into his mind, a plan that would seem crazy to a materialist, but of utmost possibility to a true believer, as Arthur had just become if he hadn't been already.

"Hi there!" a bold masculine voice suddenly said through the telephone receiver or whatever it was. "You've reached the offices of Dexter's Numinous Services, Dexter speaking. How may I help?"

"I need a god," Arthur said, gasping.

"Many of us do," Dexter said. "But what does that have to do with me?"

"I need a god to fulfill a need for me."

"I see, sir. Do you have your entry number handy?"

Arthur, on the thin crumbly edge of hysteria, heard himself say, "Entry number? I don' need no stinkin' entry number."

"I'm afraid you do, sir. Which god told you to call us?"

"I called Information and they connected me to you."

"They shouldn't have," Dexter said. "We work only for people who have had a genuine vision in which a god imparted an entry number so that he could fulfill their wish. Good-bye, sir, and have a nice—"

"Look," Arthur husked, "I'm in a jam here. I badly need a wish granted, but unfortunately I haven't had a vision that revealed an entry number. Isn't there something you can do for me?"

"I'm very sorry," Dexter said, "but we work only with authorized and authenticated entry numbers as given by one of our list of approved gods and transmitted via a genuine inspired vision. We'd risk losing our license if we dealt with you."

"But I'm desperate!"

"Desperate, sir, but not inspired. It makes all the difference, you see."

"Can you at least tell me what to do next?"

"Well, I'm not supposed to . . . "

"Please, please!"

"In your circumstances, I can only suggest that you try Godshome. It's unlikely you'll come up with anything useful there, but at least it's a try."

"I'll try it! How do I get to Godshome?"

"Just one moment and I'll transfer you."

There was a clicking sound and then the sound of a telephone ringing, then a woman's voice.

"Godshome. Nurse Hulga speaking."

"I need to talk to a god!" Arthur said, his throat becoming quite raw from his frequent gasping.

"I'm sorry, sir, none of our gods come to the telephone. It's beneath their dignity."

"But I need to *talk* to one," Arthur said.

"You would have to do that in person, here at Godshome."

"You mean I could come visit?"

"Of course," Nurse Hulga said. "There are still almost three hours of visiting time left. Could you come right away?"

"I could indeed," Arthur said. "The trouble is, I don't know how to get there."

"Oh, that's no problem. Are you calling from a touchtone phone?"

"Yes, I am."

"Then just press star-star-two-six-star."

"That's all it takes?"

"Yes. And stand close to the receiver."

This was quite mad, Arthur thought. But at least when the feds came to get him they'd find him safely crazy rather than drearily and depressingly sane. He pushed the indicated buttons and held the receiver close to his face.

There followed a whooshing sound. Arthur felt something curious, as though a small transparent octopus had been plastered to his face. He reached to pull the thing off. His hands were pulled into the invisible whatever-it-was. He started to scream as he was drawn into the telephone.

CHAPTER 5

THE MOMENT OF ARTHUR BEING PULLED INTO THE TELEPHONE was an unusual one but it didn't last very long. A moment later, or perhaps less, Arthur found himself in a strange place. It had the look of reception rooms all over the world: tan walls, linoleum floor, indirect overhead lighting with an annoying flicker.

"I wish they'd get around to fixing that," a woman's voice said.

Arthur found that he was sitting in a ladder-back chair looking across a desk at a large woman in a starched white uniform. She had a broad, no-nonsense face, a big bosom that looked in its starched white uniform like it was made of boiled steel; thick ankles, hair on the backs of her hands, and the slightest suggestion of a mustache.

"I am Nurse Hulga," she said. "You expressed a desire to visit us?"

"Yes, yes, I did," Arthur said, coming to himself with commendable alacrity. "Where am I, exactly? Just for the record, I mean."

"This is Godshome," Hulga said. "Or to be more specific, it is the Cosmos Universal Rest Home for Aged, Indigent, and Decrepit Dieties. Isn't this where you expected to come?"

"Of course," Arthur said. "I just wanted to make sure I'd come to the right place. Crossed wires can play nasty tricks sometimes."

He looked around the reception room with its institutional air of boiled cabbage. "So this is where the gods go when they're finished out there?" he said with a vague gesture and what he hoped was a knowing air.

"Yes, some of them do come here," Nurse Hulga said.

"Out of choice?" Arthur asked.

"You need to understand the situation. Some of them have been around so long they can no longer care for themselves."

"I thought gods were immortal," Arthur said.

"They are, of course. But you have to understand how it is for a diety. Earth people think that immortality means you can go on forever just as you are."

"You mean you can't?"

Hulga shook her head. "It doesn't work that way. Physically, yes, a god or goddess can continue indefinitely. It's built into the situation. But mentally—psychologically—you must realize that being a god takes a terrible toll."

Arthur nodded. "All that horsing around in heaven?" he suggested.

Hulga gave him a severe look. "There's a lot more to it than that. When you're a god, people's thoughts, hopes, dreams, and fears are beating at you all the time. Gods have direct apprehension of the feelings of their worshippers. It can be taxing."

"I didn't know that," Arthur said.

"After a while all those prayers and petitions from humans take their toll. It's all very well at the beginning. Most gods, even the compassionate ones, just let it all roll over them. But after a while it gets to even the toughest. They get sick of the daily drudgery of hearing desperate pleas, and, in most cases, being unable to do very much about them."

"That's new to me," Arthur said. "I thought a god could do anything."

"In theory, yes. But in actual fact, a god's power is circumscribed by the power of other gods, and by the Fair Faith Among Dieties Act which stipulates that any god must accept the ruling of any other god in respect to humanity. And a god's power is also limited by the inner premise of the human situation."

"What is the inner premise of the human situation?" Arthur asked.

Hulga frowned. "I thought everyone knew that. The inner premise states that, with few exceptions, people have to take what comes to them, bear up to it, or fall down under it."

"That's the inner premise of the human situation?"

"That's it."

"And then the humans die," Arthur said, unable to work up much sympathy for the gods.

"Yes, they die, and in distressingly brief times from the viewpoint of a god."

"That must be real tough on a god, having his worshippers die on him."

Hulga didn't register his sarcasm. "Gods live in longer lines than mortals. It takes them longer to do things. By the time something comes to a god's attention, and by the time he decides to do something about it, the human most likely is dead and buried. It's frustrating for a god, having to work in such a short time frame."

"Amazing they get anything at all done for people," Arthur said.

"They try their best, most of them. But remember, gods can make exceptions for only a very few. A god has a lot more on his mind than the troubles of his constituents. It would be fair to say that most gods end up hating humans because they're so needy, always with the hand out, always with the gimme, gimme."

"Yes, I suppose so," Arthur said, feeling uncomfortable but still wanting what he wanted, namely, a miraculous rescue that ought to be perfectly simple for a god.

"In any event," Hulga said, "it's good of you to want to visit the ones we have here in Godshome. Their own relatives are shockingly remiss in that regard. You'll find one or two of the dears on the porch and the rest on the lawn. Feel free to talk to whoever you wish. They're really very sweet. Just go out the door and straight ahead. I'll telephone you back to Earth when you're ready to leave."

Arthur went out of the reception room, still feeling somewhat tentative but determined to see this through. He proceeded through a large ballroom with folding chairs stacked against one wall and an empty bandstand with a sign reading ZIGGY STARLIGHT'S HEAVENLY TRIO WILL PERFORM AT NINE TONIGHT UNIVERSAL SIDEREAL TIME. He continued through sliding doors onto a glassed-in porch. Beyond the glass he caught a glimpse of a green lawn with what looked like a cocker spaniel frolicking about, and figures in wheelchairs dotted here and there. But his attention was taken by the sight of one old man, wrapped in a plaid shawl, sitting not five feet from him on the veranda and rocking slowly in a big rocker while he gazed morosely into the middle distance.

Arthur approached him, his pulse racing. This was the first god he had ever encountered face-to-face.

The god must have been a big fellow in his prime. He still had the bold features of a Roman emperor or a classical actor. But now he had a shrunken, hump-backed look, as of some once-noble building that had collapsed in on itself. This god didn't look up when Arthur approached and coughed in a tentative manner. Arthur noticed that the god was watching a small black-and-white television on whose screen young ladies in white gauze with wings floated through an insipid aerial ballet.

"Er, I beg your pardon," Arthur said.

The god turned his majestic head and frowned. "Yers? Whazzit?"

Arthur noticed that on a little table beside the rocking chair was a large brown bottle labeled SOMA — TO BE USED FOR MEDICINAL PURPOSES ONLY. He suspected the god was intoxicated. Nevertheless, he cleared his throat and made his pitch.

"I'm a stranger around here," Arthur began, vaguely enough, "and I'd like to ask—"

"You a god?" the god asked abruptly.

"No. As a matter of fact, I'm a mortal."

"Thought as much. I'm a god, you know."

"Yes. I could see that right away."

"Actually, I'm the only real god in this place. The rest of them are just a pack of jumped-up demons. I shouldn't be here, you know."

"No?" Arthur said, in what he hoped was a winning manner.

"No. I happen to be a lot more than just a god. I'm lord of the universe." He fixed Arthur with a fierce glare. "What do you think of that?"

"Impressive," Arthur said.

"But my jealous relatives have put me away here so they can play around with the women. What do you think of that?"

"Shocking," Arthur said.

"Nothing shocking about it," the god said. "Playing around with the women is what god relatives do. What's shocking is them deposing me from my throne and sticking me in here to vegetate with a bunch of jumped-up demons."

"That's really a pity," Arthur said. And then, seeing a place to put in his pitch, said, "But I've come here to offer you a chance to get back into action."

"Eh? What was that?" The god cupped a hand behind his ear. "Don't hear so good, you know."

"A chance to get back into action," Arthur said, louder.

"Action? What d'you mean, action?"

"Back into the human world. An opportunity to do a good deed. Grant a wish. That sort of thing."

"Back into the world?" the old god said. "Boy, you must be a lot sillier than you look to think I'd ever go back to godding it. It's god eat god out there, and I've had enough. Don't an old god deserve his rest? Don't he?"

"Of course," Arthur said hastily. "I just thought that since you said—"

"Pay no attention," the old god said. "I'm delusional. Ain't that plain to see?"

"If you're delusional," Arthur said, "how do you happen to know it? I thought the condition would be self-deceiving, so to speak."

"Don't be a snot nose," the old god said.

"Sorry," Arthur said.

"I can have my moments of unbearable clarity like anyone else," the old god said.

"Of course," Arthur said.

"Now get away from me, boy, before I break your back. The temerity! Asking me, the only real god in this stupid place, to subject myself once again to the slings and arrows of outrageous—outrageous—"

"Fortune?" Arthur suggested.

The god stared at him for a while, then said, "Get away from me while you still can, wiseass. You might try one of the others with your proposition, though I doubt very much any-one in here is crazy enough to accede to your selfish demands."

"Yes, sir, sorry, sir, I'll just nip along then," Arthur said, and hastily walked to the door that led out to the green grass, opened it, and passed outside.

The grounds he walked on were lushly grassed and neatly clipped. The cocker spaniel barked twice, sharply, and ran

around the side of the building out of sight. Arthur stepped
onto a flagstoned path that led between water sprinklers to a
jolly little gazebo. Sitting in it was a very large god in pale
green hospital pajamas and wearing a tam o'shanter. This god
was reclined in a recliner. Plastic tubes poked out of the side
of his neck. He gave Arthur a civil little nod.

"Nice day," Arthur hazarded.

"Just like all the others," the god said.

"Yes. But that must be nice."

"I suppose it would be, if anyone around here gave a shit
about nice."

"Yes, that's so true," Arthur said.

The large god squinted at him. "Mortal?"

"As a matter of fact, yes," Arthur said. "God?"

"Of course."

"Had an injury?" Arthur asked, glancing at the plastic tub-
ing which ran into a small machine that huffed in a muffled
manner.

"Kidney failure," the god said succinctly.

"I didn't think gods were subject to mortal pains," Arthur
said.

"We're not. But there's such a thing as psychosomatic ill-
ness, you know."

"Of course." Arthur cleared his throat several times, then
said, "I don't suppose you'd like to get out of here, would you?"

"No. Why should I?"

"Well, you could return to all your olden glories, as the
poet said."

"Which poet was that?"

"I don't quite remember."

"I remember everything," the god said. "Even at its best it
wasn't so great. People write a lot of bullshit about the pleasures of godding it."

"There must have been some satisfactory moments."

The god glared at him. "What the hell do you know about it?"

"Oh, nothing, less than nothing," Arthur said. "I was just conjecturing. I was just wondering . . . "

"What?"

"Well, I was wondering if you might not like to get back into action. I've got a great way for you to begin."

"And what is that?"

"You could perform a miracle for me. I'd be ever so grateful."

"Hah!" the god snorted.

"I beg pardon?"

"I said, 'Hah!' "

"That's what I thought you said. And does it mean what I think it means?"

"What do you think it means?"

"That you're not interested."

"You got it," the large god said. "If you think any god in this place is interested in going back into the hustle and bustle of a working god's life, you're even stupider than you look."

"I didn't mean to give offense," Arthur said.

"Don't worry about it. You'll be dead before I get around to working up much of a head of steam over it."

With that discomforting thought, Arthur moved on down the path. On either side of him, scattered around the green lawns, he saw other gods and some goddesses, too, reclining on recliners or lying on chaise longues and staring into space. They looked so old, stern, and forbidding that he didn't have the heart to disturb them.

He continued along the walk until he came to a wall of soft white stuff. It seemed to be some kind of a mist. He was about to step into it when a voice said sharply, "Hey, you there! Watch your step!"

Arthur stopped and turned. He saw a tall, very thin man in gray overalls and a green wool shirt pushing a trash can mounted on wheels.

"I'm sorry," Arthur said. "Am I not supposed to go there?"

"You can go where you like," the man said, "but if you continue that way you'll fall over the edge."

"The edge?"

"That's right, the edge. And it's a long way to solid ground."

Arthur looked into the mist. It parted for a moment and he saw that the lawn ended as abruptly as if it had been sheered, and beyond the edge was nothing but the empty azure of limitless sky.

Arthur stepped back. "There isn't even a guard rail!"

"The people around here don't need one."

"Are you a god?"

"Not bloody likely," the tall man said. "I'm the ground-keeper."

"Is that a gardener?"

"You might say so."

Arthur peered over the edge again. He saw that the grass rested on a solid bank of cloud.

"What makes it look so solid?" Arthur asked.

"It doesn't happen by itself," the groundkeeper said. "I spray it twice a week with E-Fix."

"E-Fix?"

"Ephemeral Fix. The stuff that makes the transitory permanent, or as close to it as one cares to come. Are you a new god?"

"No," Arthur said dully. "I'm a mortal, and I'm going home now."

Sadly he walked back to the rest home. He was ready to take Nurse Hulga up on her offer to telephone him back home. It had all been extremely depressing, this talking with the gods, and a real blow for one who had been a bit of an idealist about dieties. There were other gods out there on the grass, but Arthur had a strong feeling he'd get no more favorable answer from them than he'd received already.

He came back onto the porch, went past the god with the Roman emperor features, who didn't look up as he passed, and entered the ballroom.

He was ready to throw in the sponge, go back and face the cops, the FBI, the court, the judge, the warden at Raiford, the other prisoners, and the rock pile, when he heard what sounded very much like a voice: "Hssst."

He looked around. No one there. He was about to resume his dolorous walk to the reception room when he heard the voice again. This time, clearly and recognizably, "Hssst."

Arthur turned again, slowly. Still no one there.

"Did someone call?"

"Yes," a voice said to him. "I did."

"Who are you?"

"Leafie's the name. Godhead's the game."

"Why can't I see you? Are you invisible?"

"Don't be a goonie," the voice said. "I'm throwing my voice."

"Oh. Where are you throwing it from?"

"Turn left, go through the door, continue to the end of the corridor, and then turn to your right."

Arthur did so, and found a set of stairs leading upward.

"Now what?"

"Come up the stairs."

"Is it allowed?"

"Hey, I'm a god and I'm telling you to do it. What more do you want?"

Arthur went up the stairs, down a short corridor, and came to a door. There was a sign on the door: WARNING! PROCEED NO FURTHER! WARD O FOR BIPOLAR CONDITIONS. OCCUPANTS MAY BE VIOLENT.

Arthur stopped. "It says I shouldn't go on."

"Well, I'm telling you to ignore that and come on in."

"It says it could be dangerous."

"Look, buddy," the voice said, sounding testy now, "it's dangerous to get out of bed in the morning. Are you a mortal in a desperate situation or are you not?"

"Well, yes, actually, I am."

"Then come in here. This is your last resort, babe. But of course, it's up to you."

Arthur hesitated, thought about the rock pile, gritted his teeth, and pushed the door open.

Beyond was a long corridor.

The voice said, "I'm down at the end. Last door on your left."

Arthur proceeded, moving slowly, but moving.

CHAPTER 6

IN APPEARANCE, LEAFIE WAS AN OLDISH BOY OR YOUNGISH man. Short and muscular, he had yellow-brown hair with a touch of russet. He was wearing a suit of leaves, mostly green ones, grape leaves, so it seemed to Arthur, and grape vines were twined around his waist and shoulders. He had a narrow clever face, large brilliant eyes, and a long thin mouth twisted into a smile.

Even more surprising than Leafie, however, was his room. It looked very much like a grotto in a woody setting, and it was a lot larger than it had any right to be. Within the woody setting, Arthur made out at least an acre of green meadow ending in a romantic grotto slanting down into the earth and from which rose mephitic vapors. At the entrance to the grotto was a small statue with an altar before it. The flayed and decomposing body of some small unidentifiable animal was rotting on the altar, and buzzing flies hovered around it.

"How'd you get all that in here?" Arthur asked.

Leafie shruged. "Magic, of course. Everybody here decorates their room as they like."

"I like your altar," Arthur said.

"It *is* nice, isn't it?"

"And your leaf suit is nice, too. You wouldn't happen to be the Great God Pan by any chance, would you?"

"That imposter? No, I'm not Pan, And I'm not Bacchus, I'm not Silenus or any of those Graeco-Roman pastoral gods. I'm Leafie, the premier god of the Dardanian Scythians."

"I don't remember reading anything about that group."

"They were an unfortunate people. No sooner had they put together a modest pantheon with me at its head than they were destroyed to a man by Cyrus the Great."

"I don't remember reading about that."

"Wiping out the Dardanian Scythians was so small an incident for Cyrus that his historians didn't even bother to record it. But it sure played hell with my plans."

"Couldn't you arrange to be worshipped by some other people?"

"I never got a chance. Pan was brought in by the Hellenes and there was no place for another god of mirth, merriment, drunkenness, and sacred frenzy such as yours truly. The duplication of gods is quite a problem. Many are called but few are chosen."

"I'm sorry to hear it. It must have been disappointing."

"Believe it. My function taken over, my worshippers destroyed . . . well, it put me into quite a state."

"I can imagine. So you came here?"

"Not of my own free will. Actually, I was sent to this place by a hangman's jury of my peers—the so-called healing gods. Asklepios and that lot. They said I was getting too excited and needed a little rest."

"Rest? From what?"

Leafie smiled a self-deprecating smile. "When my last worshipper was killed, I got into a bit of a state. It was just boyish excitement, combined with disappointment at losing my place in what had promised to be a really first-rate pantheon. I even had a chance to fit into the Egyptian thing—Ammon and Isis and those. They said they needed a really good trickster god. But before anything was decided, I got shipped off here. Frankly, I was oxcarted."

"Oxcarted?"

"I believe you would call it railroaded."

"I'm sorry to hear about it," Arthur said. "I know how you feel. I've got a few difficulties myself."

"Indeed? Tell me about them."

Arthur told Leafie about the gold mine and his investment in it. He began to explain about selling short, but Leafie interrupted him.

"I know about that. We did that on the old Babylonian exchange."

"Well, I have to pay up in a few days. I owe a lot of money. I need a miracle to get out of trouble."

"You want the main stockholders killed?"

"Nothing as serious as that. You see, this gold mine I was telling you about is right beside a volcano. If someone could break through the underground wall that separates the mine from the molten lava, that would do the trick and no one would be hurt."

"No one? What about the people who bought stock in the mine?"

"They were mostly anticipating it failing."

"I see," Leafie said. "A crime without a victim, eh?"

"I'd prefer to think of it as an act of a god with only good consequences for most people."

"Well, it's a neat scheme," Leafie said. "Really a job for a chthonic diety. But I think I could handle it without too much trouble and a little help from my friends."

"Could you? Would you?"

"Could isn't any problem. The question is, will I?"

"And what is the answer?"

"We might be able to come to an arrangement. But there would be certain conditions."

"Name them!"

"You would need to worship me, of course."

"No problem. I practically worship you already."

"And there would be certain other conditions. You'd have to grant me the right to operate on Earth in any capacity I saw fit, and for as long as I wanted. With that would go the right to do anything I deemed proper, and in whatever manner I chose. I'd also need the right to subcontract work. You would have to grant me these rights in perpetuity and to promise never to rescind our agreement, never to repudiate me."

Arthur knew a moment of fear.

"Do I even have the power to grant these rights?"

"You're a full-blooded human, aren't you?"

"Of course."

"Then you've got the power to grant rights to petitioning dieties."

"Is that really how it's done?"

"How do you think the others came to Earth?"

"I never thought about it."

"Some worshipper asked them in, that's how."

"And what do I get in return?"

"What you need. I will turn the aforesaid gold mine into a slag of molten lava which no one will work for generations to come."

"That's what I need, all right," Arthur said.

"Then do we have a deal?"

Arthur had the feeling he was getting in deeper than he'd expected. But there seemed nothing he could do about it if he wanted Leafie's services. And Leafie seemed quite a reasonable sort of diety, a little wild, perhaps, but quite sympathetic.

"I guess I can go along with all that," Arthur said.

"I may think of a few more points," Leafie said. "I'll draw them up in a document and you can sign it."

"Is that really necessary?"

"Oh yes. You can never tell when one of the High Gods may want to review the matter."

"Who are the High Gods?" Arthur asked.

"Just a bunch of jumped-up dieties who think that because they have power they deserve respect. Don't bother your head about them. It's pretty much of an internal affair. Come on, we'll go downstairs and have Nurse Hulga type this up for us."

Arthur had the feeling that events were moving just a little too quickly for him to grasp. But he needed quick action to save him from the consequences of his inconsidered action back on Earth, so he decided to raise no objections.

They went down to Nurse Hulga's reception room, where Leafie explained that he was doing a contract with Arthur.

"Does this mean you'll be leaving us, Leafie?" Nurse Hulga asked.

"It does indeed," Leafie said. "I want to thank you for all the help you've given me. I feel much better now. I don't get those weird mood swings anymore."

"The doctors thought you should really stay a few centuries more to be sure we've stabilized your condition."

"Hey, I've never felt better in my life!"

"I really don't recommend your leaving us at this time."

"Just roll a sheet of parchment into your typewriter and take down what I dictate. I'll be the judge of my own condition, thank you very much."

Nurse Hulga turned to Arthur. "Are you sure you want to do this?"

"He's sure, he's sure," Leafie said. "Aren't you, Arthur?"

"I guess I am," Arthur said. "I'm in quite a difficult position, you see—"

"Let's get on with it," Leafie said. "Hulga, take this down: 'I, Arthur Fenn, being a full-blooded human being of sound mind and fully capable of entering into this agreement, do grant to Leafie, diety at large, the following terms in perpetuity . . . "

There followed a list of items, all the ones they had discussed in Leafie's room and several that hadn't been mentioned. Arthur wondered about those, but held his peace. It was important to get on with this while the god was in a good mood.

At last it was done. Arthur signed with a stylus Hulga gave him, and Leafie followed with his signature.

"That's it!" Leafie said, folding the parchment and stowing it in a sort of branch-and-moss backpack attached to his shoulders by vine tendrils. "We're practically on our way! I'm sure Nurse Hulga won't mind telephoning you back home. I'll catch up with you in a little while. There are a few things I need to put together first."

"You won't forget? I've got less than three days before my commitment is due."

"Hey, babe," Leafie said, "don't worry, we got ourselves an agreement. We're going to be seeing a lot of each other, believe me."

"If you're quite ready," Nurse Hulga said, her pursed lips showing just what she thought of the arrangements.

"I'm ready," Arthur said. "Please telephone me home." And she did.

CHAPTER 7

UPON RETURNING BY TELEPHONE FROM GODSHOME TO HIS
own home, Arthur fell into bed, too tired to consider the ram-
ifications of what he had done.

When he awoke the next morning, he wondered if the
whole thing had not been an inexplicable dream.

He was halfway through his first cup of coffee when the
telephone rang. It was Sammy.

"Arthur, I've got wonderful news. The big old volcano
blew its top last night. There's a dust cloud you can see all the
way from Rio."

"And what about the mine?"

"The mine is kaput, dear boy. Where there had been a big
operation, now there's a lake of hardening lava."

"I hope nobody was hurt . . . "

"Are you kidding? This thing wiped out five native vil-
lages, couple hundred Indians killed, to say nothing of fifty or
so mine company personnel."

"Oh, dear."

"Yeah, a tragedy, isn't it? But there's no loss without some
gain. You're the gainer, Arthur. The price of those shares you
bought short has fallen deliciously."

"I'm surprised they're still traded at all."

"The company claims it has a process for doing something with lava. But it'll never work."

"So I'm out of the hole?"

"You're out of it and well up the other side. At this point your investment is worth a conservative fifty-eight thousand dollars."

"Okay. Sell."

"Are you sure? The price is sure to drop even farther."

"I'm sure. Sell me out. Sammy, this is not my game."

"Okay, buddy, sell it is. Come down to the office tomorrow, sign a few papers, and we'll give you a check."

"As easy as that?"

"Just that easy, babe."

"Oh, Sammy . . . did they have any idea why the volcano blew at this time?"

"Not a clue. I told you, nobody knows why volcanoes do what they do. Act of God, I suppose."

CHAPTER 8

THE NEXT FEW DAYS WERE QUIET ONES FOR ARTHUR FENN.
The events at Godshome had begun to fade from his memory.
He had even started to lose his guilt over the people he'd
killed by calling up Leafie and having him set off the volcano.
He rationalized it by convincing himself that Leafie probably
had nothing to do with it. Maybe the whole thing had just
been an accident, the luck of the draw . . . for who can tell
when a volcano is going to blow, as Sammy so sagely said?

Then Leafie came to visit.

It happened one evening while Arthur sat watching a glorious sunset from his veranda. He watched it somewhat
guiltily, because the newspapers said the recent splendid sun-
sets were caused by dust thrown in the air caused by the volcano erupting in Brazil. His fault. Still, he had to live with it.
And it *was* a pretty sunset.

He was just about to go to bed when whammo, there was
Leafie, standing on his veranda bold as brass in his skin/cloth-
ing of leaves and vines.

"Hi there, old buddy," Leafie said.

"Oh, hi." Arthur looked around. "Let's talk inside."

He led Leafie into his living room, gave him a beer, and
settled him in the best chair.

"How you doin'?" Leafie asked.

"I'm just fine."

"How'd you like that volcano thing?"

"You did that?"

Leafie took a swig of beer and smiled with satisfaction. "You don't think it happened all by itself, do you?"

"Well, after all, I didn't know."

"Didn't expect me to sign my name to it, did you?"

"I suppose not."

"As a matter of fact, I needed some help on this one. That little gap you were talking about between the volcano and the mine? It turned out to be twenty-five feet of solid rock. You don't tear those things down as easy as that, not even if you're a god."

"What did you do?"

"I called on a couple of my friends."

"Anyone I might have met? I did talk to several gods in Godshome."

"That crew of old timers? Don't make me laugh. My friends don't hang out in a place like that. I got friends among the gods, baby, but they're not farting around any old gods' home."

"Where are they?"

"That's a little difficult to explain. When there's no work for a god, he needs a place to hang out until someone can use him. My friends were in a place we call Cthuluville."

"Interesting name," Arthur said.

"It's where they pack the incorrigibles. The gods who just don't fit in. That's where they had me before they sent me to Godshome for rehabilitation."

Leafie hadn't mentioned rehabilitation before. But now didn't seem the time to ask him about it.

Arthur said, "I want to thank you very much for all you've done for me. I'll look forward to visiting with you one of these days. But now I suppose you've got a lot of things to do . . . "

"Hey, buddy, what is this? The old brush-off?"

"Not at all. It's just that we've done what we set out to do . . . "

"What *you* set out to do. What *I* want to do is just beginning. We got a new day coming, you and me."

"Actually, I'm not feeling quite up to anything just now."

"You got the blues, buddy? I'll give you a dose of soma; medicine of the gods, it'll fix you right up."

"I think I just need a period of rest and solitude and absolute quiet . . . "

"Hey, don't be a goony. I've got plans for us, baby. How many rooms you got here?"

"It's only a small cottage. Two bedrooms, the living room, Florida room, kitchenette, and the garage."

"That'll do for a start. I'll use the spare bedroom for me and my pals until we work out something better."

"Pals? What pals?"

"I told you, I got a couple of other gods to help set off the volcano. I had to promise them something, didn't I?"

"Why should they want to stay in my spare bedroom?"

"Because it's a start."

"A start for what?"

"For some plans I got regarding Earth. Glad you asked us here, Arthur. I haven't had much of a chance to look around, but it seems a nice place."

"What are you planning?"

"Relax, buddy, you'll see. Big plans! And we're going to build the whole thing around you. Why don't you move your crap out of that spare bedroom? A couple of my friends ought to be arriving soon. Tell 'em I'll be back."

"Where are you going?"

"Out to take a look around."

Arthur managed to convince Leafy that his leaf outfit might bring unwanted attention. Arthur had a pair of Levi's and a polo shirt that fit the diety nicely. With these and a pair of soft moccasins, and ten dollars for walking-around money, Leafie was all set, and he left the bungalow whistling.

The first diety showed up less than ten minutes later. She appeared in Arthur's living room in a puff of bile-scented smoke. She was short and very broad, with a misshapen turnip head and feet like tree roots.

"Hi," she said. "I'm Luuma. That's with two u's. You must be Arthur."

"Pleased to meet you," Arthur said. He offered his hand to Luuma, but she grabbed him with her two long, skinny, hairy arms and gave him a bone-bending hug.

"Arthur," she said, "I can't tell you how happy I am to be here. You have no idea what a shithouse Cthuluville is."

Luuma told him that she had had a brief reign as goddess of death by torture for the Lumerian Askleps, a Mongol tribe whose practices had been so atrocious that all the tribes in the region got together and wiped them out to the last man, woman, and child, not even sparing the dogs.

Luuma's head had evolved from her sloping shoulders without benefit of a neck. Her mouth was wide and flabby with big pointed yellow teeth visible behind loose flappy lips. She had little pig eyes and a big Roman nose. Her hair looked like a mass of fine black wires that had been passed through a crinkler. She wore a rotting leopard skin off one shoulder which came down to her scabby knees.

"Leafie said the spare bedroom," she said. "Let's check it out."

Arthur took her to the room, which he had neatened up. Luuma bounced on the bed, said it would do just fine until they could come up with something better.

"I'm going to take a snooze," she said. "It's tiring, getting from Cthuluville and having to duck the High Gods all the way."

"Oh? Are the High Gods looking for you?"

"Not yet. But they don't like to see anyone get out of Cthu-luville. They'd send me back if they caught me."

"Aren't they apt to find you here?"

"It wouldn't matter. I'm on a legitimate human planet in-vited by a legitimate human."

"Actually," Arthur said, "I don't remember inviting you."

"You invited Leafie and his friends. That takes care of the letter of the law."

The next to arrive was Yah, god of infanticide. He was tall and skinny, his bones barely held together by a membrane of nearly transparent skin. His nose was so long it came down over his mouth like the flap of an envelope, causing Yah to engage in considerable maneuvers when he fed, which was frequently. He was a diety of the Lanolian Turks, a small pre-Seljik tribe whose practice of obligatory infanticide had wiped out their race before it ever got started. Yah was glad to get out of Cthuluville, and back, as he expressed it, "into ac-tion." He said the spare bedroom suited him fine, and he piled in on top of snoring Luuma, to take a nap before the fun began.

The last to arrive that evening was Rotte, god of treach-erous warfare of the pre-Columbian Otumis, who had been wiped out by the Olmec tribe in a victory celebrated all over Mexico by the tribes who had had enough of the Otumis's sly and murderous ways. The Otumis had been a large tribe, but their habit of invariably breaking their word had rendered their plans transparent to opposing tribes who tried to make agreements with them, and they had been exterminated de-spite all their gods' efforts on their behalf.

Rotte had the shape of an old man. His features were con-siderably disarranged, however. His mouth was on the top of his bald head, his eyes were on his fingertips, and he carried his stomach slung over one shoulder.

Like the others, he expressed his pleasure at being back

in a place where he could "make a difference," and piled into the bedroom on top of the other two sleeping dieties.

It was apparent that these gods were used to sleeping rough. Leafie arrived after this and, after wishing Arthur a good night, piled in on top of the other three, straining the bed but not quite breaking it. Arthur retired to his own bedroom, where he was kept awake for hours by the dreadful squashy sounds of the gods engaged in their horrid fornications. At last, just before dawn, he fell into a troubled slumber. His last thought was how good it would be once Leafie got his act together and took himself and these other dieties to some place that would better suit their swinish proclivities.

CHAPTER 9

BUT LEAFIE AND HIS FELLOW GODS SEEMED IN NO RUSH TO leave. They hung around the cottage all day drinking beer, which Arthur supplied, and talking over their plans. Among themselves they talked in Godalong, one of the dialects of the lower gods, and Arthur couldn't understand what they were saying.

Arthur disliked the whole thing intensely. But there didn't seem to be anything he could do about it. He spent the day away from his home in the Tahiti Beach public library, absentmindedly turning the pages of magazines, in a daze.

He came out of it in the early afternoon, remembering that he had to pick up his check at Sammy's stock brokerage house.

When he entered, Sammy gave him a broad smile, and one of the partners, Mr. Tripp, was also on hand to greet him. Tripp was smiling, too, but not quite as broadly. In fact, an impartial witness might have detected the least bit of strain around the corners of that smile.

"Mr. Gluck told me about your coup," Tripp said, offering his hand. "My congratulations on a most remarkable piece of business. You don't happen to have any friends in the gold mining business, do you? Or any associates who are experts in vulcanology?"

"No, I don't," Arthur said. "Why? Would it matter if I did?"

"Not to me, of course," Tripp said. "But the SEC might be interested if such were the case."

"I beg your pardon?"

"The Securities and Exchange Commission. They have taken an interest in this."

"You mean they think I did something wrong?"

"Not at all!" Tripp said, with too hearty a laugh. "But whenever there's an enormous and unexpected change in a stock's position, they're apt to wonder just why it all happened the way it did. That's understandable, isn't it? It was a most unusual coup."

"I wish I'd been in on it myself," Sammy said. "I almost was, but I couldn't get my order down in time."

"What should I do?" Arthur asked.

"There's nothing for you to do. If the SEC have any questions, they'll be in touch." Tripp laughed again, hollowly. "I don't suppose you were planning any long trips in the near future, were you?"

"No . . . do I need a lawyer?"

"Plenty of time for that later, if it comes to that. It probably won't. There's really no need to concern yourself."

"Maybe I shouldn't spend any of the money yet," Arthur said.

"I was just coming to that," Tripp said. "Sammy, perhaps you'd care to explain this part."

"Sure," Sammy said. "Look at it this way, Arthur. There's good news and there's bad news. The good news is that your original twenty-two-thousand-dollar investment, which grew to fifty-eight thousand yesterday, appreciated to approximately three hundred thousand before the SEC suspended trading in the stock."

"And the bad news?"

"All transactions pertaining to Amalgamated Mining of Bahia have been frozen pending the outcome of the SEC's investigation. That means our company's position is frozen, too, Arthur. We're all going to have to wait until the SEC get finished."

"I don't suppose you could just give me back my twenty-two thousand and we could forget about the whole thing?"

"We can't do that, of course," Mr. Tripp said. "But don't be disheartened, Mr. Fenn. Potentially, you are a wealthy man. And I'm sure the SEC will find you blameless in this matter."

There was more handshaking and more smiles. Sammy walked Arthur to the door. "I'll come around as soon as I can," Sammy said. "We'll talk. Don't be upset. This is going to work out just fine."

"I hope you're right," Arthur said. "When you come over, you're going to see something a bit unusual."

"What's that? Been making some purchases on credit?"

Arthur decided it was impossible to explain. "You'll see. Later, Sammy."

He hurried home. He'd just remembered he had a household of hungry gods to feed. And no money to do it with.

Leafie had anticipated the money problem. He and the other gods had brought along chunks of gold ore from Godsrealm, where there seemed to be plenty of gold around but nowhere to spend it. Arthur took the ore to the assay office in the nearby city of Orlandita and converted it to cash. With this he was able to buy the supplies they needed: whole chickens, rabbits, and sheep. The gods like to eat their food raw. Arthur pleaded with them to try some regular cooked food, but they stuck to their preferences.

He was afraid this was going to cause trouble, and sure enough, that evening a cop came to the door and told Arthur his neighbors were accusing him of running a slaughterhouse in an area zoned for residential living. And in fact the yard was littered with large, well-gnawed bones. Arthur promised he'd clean it up.

The cop was curious as to just what was going on inside.

"You got some people staying here?"

"Friends of the family. They're just here for a little while."

"You aren't hiding illegals by any chance, are you?"

"No, not me."

"I think I'd better meet these relatives of yours."

"They're sleeping."

"So wake them up."

"Couldn't we do this some other time?"

"Buddy, I said now."

Arthur went into the bedroom, where the gods were sleeping in a noisome tangle. He woke them up. They got out of bed, uncoiling themselves from around one another. Finally, Luuma pulled on a pink petticoat and said, "I'll talk to this guy."

"Maybe you'd better not. We don't want any trouble."

She gave him a grin. "We *like* trouble."

When she came out, bloated and inhuman-looking, the officer goggled at her, unable to believe his eyes.

"So what's the beef?" Luuma asked.

"I need to see your papers."

"Oh you do, do you?" She gave him a lascivious leer. "I can show you a lot more than a bunch of silly old papers, cutie."

"Just the papers," the cop said, his hand on the butt of his gun, backing away.

She reached out a skinny, hairy arm and grabbed him by the throat. "Listen, pal," she said, "if I was you I'd just forget about all this. You know what I mean?"

"Argggh," the cop said, strangling.

"Because if you want trouble, we got a world of it waiting for you here."

She fixed him with baleful eyes. Ominous flickering lights

shone from them. The cop was unable to repress a whimper. She shook him like a rat, then pushed him away.

"You get the idea?" She shook him again, released him, and went back inside.

The cop, badly shaken, straightened his uniform and looked at Arthur.

"What was that?"

"What was what?" Arthur asked.

"That thing."

"I didn't see anything," Arthur said. "Do you feel all right, officer?"

The officer gave a long shudder, and pulling himself together, muttered, "There's something going on here and I don't want to know about it. No more animals on the premises unless you got a license. You hear me?"

"I hear you," Arthur said.

"Don't let it happen again. I really don't want to have to come back here. You know what I mean?"

"I know," Arthur said. "I sympathize."

The cop went back to his police car and drove off, slowly at first, then with increasing speed.

CHAPTER 10

WITH FOUR UNRULY GODS IN HIS HOUSE, ARTHUR'S LIFE changed from unpredictable to downright chaotic. Food was the gods' preoccupation and they liked it alive, bloody, and plentiful. Arthur pleaded with them to leave the neighborhood animals alone. They complied by going farther afield, raiding throughout the county to bring in the dogs, cats, pigs, chickens, sheep, and goats that made up their preferred diet. But despite their best efforts, these gods seemed unable to differentiate between strays and household pets. Animals continued to be carried into Arthur's house in the small hours of the night, and either eaten raw or plopped into Arthur's big spaghetti pot to soften them up a bit.

This sort of thing didn't pass unnoticed. There were articles in the local newspapers regarding the sudden increase in cattle rustling and animal thievery throughout Magnolia County and extending into Broward and Dade. Leafie went back to wherever he had come from and brought in some more bullion. Arthur converted it into money, and, after a little experimentation, bought blood sausage by the fifty-pound case. The gods devoured it raw. They also liked chorizo, uncooked, and Arthur put in a special order with a nearby Mexican food specialty house for daily orders of the stuff.

Food wasn't the only expense. The gods also needed clothing, and they demanded quantities of semiprecious stones with which to adorn the altars they raised to themselves in various corners of the house. Arthur paid for all this after the gods soon ran out of gold bullion. Arthur soon felt the pinch. The money from the gold ore was all used up, and his check for the gold short-selling was delayed pending an investigation into possible price-fixing of the stock.

During this period, Arthur's fiancée dropped over. Mimi was small, with mousy brown hair, not much in the way of calves, and a modest bosom. On the day of her visit, she wore a starched, frilly blouse and straight skirt with patent leather pumps of simple but classic design.

Mimi and Arthur had met in the big Saks outlet store in the Tahiti Beach mall. An aunt had given Arthur a fifty-dollar gift certificate for his birthday and he'd gone to Saks to see how he could spend it. Nothing seemed to be in his price range, so he'd gone to the main counter to ask if he could return the certificate for cash.

Mimi was working on the service desk. She told him that it wasn't store policy to give cash for certificates, but suggested he buy a necktie. Arthur said he hardly ever wore one and wouldn't know how to pick one out. Mimi accompanied him to the tie counter and picked out a composition in salmon pink and sulphur yellow. She said it went with his complexion. Arthur thanked her, thinking it was a compliment.

Afterward, they went for a coffee and talked. He admired Mimi's air of class. She liked his appearance of malleability, so important if you expect to train a man to be a good provider. She was petite, with small, pretty kewpie-doll features. He was tall and stooped, with the look of a shambling young Abe Lincoln in his unfocused stage before he came up with the genius idea of saving his country and freeing the slaves. Class and character, with malleability as the main ingredient. What a couple they'd make! How could they miss?

They started to date. He liked her air of near-unap-
proachability. In this age of promiscuous women who were
frightening in their lusts, at least as portrayed in movies, it
showed that she was well brought up. She admired his height:
tall gaunt men were said to do better in business than their
shorter more rotund compatriots, at least according to *Psy-
chology Today*.

Their families, if not exactly dancing with joy, at least tolerated their choices, having given up on each of them years
earlier, though for different reasons. Mimi, twenty, with two
years of finishing school in Palm Beach, wanted to get out of
her parents' house and furnish her own place already. Arthur,
twenty-seven, with a degree in comparative mythology, wanted
a wife to bustle around the cottage he had inherited from his
parents.

Arthur bought Mimi an engagement ring with a small off-
white diamond, this through Sammy, who had contacts for
everything. Mimi thought it looked nice on her small hand.
They announced their engagement, but got vague when people asked when they were going to set a date.

As she got to know Arthur better, Mimi began to suspect
that he wasn't really as malleable as he looked. Arthur always
aimed to please, but he had a deep-seated diffidence and lack
of drive that became increasingly apparent as the weeks and
months passed. As for Mimi, although she was dainty and
pretty and had wonderful manners, she also had a deep-seated
mean streak that was difficult to hide. Sammy, who was not
judgmental but fancied himself a comedian, and observing
her back-slanting forehead and undershot jaw with the two
tiny front teeth protruding daintily, likened her to an attack
ferret in high heels. Arthur was not amused. He thought she
was beautiful. He recognized that he and Mimi were in some
ways a mismatch, but he loved her, and more to the point, he
desired her. Not that it did him any good: Mimi had ruled

there would be no hanky panky, as she called the supreme act between a man and a woman, until the knot was tied.

Their situation had been a little strained of late, as Mimi had come to realize that holders of doctorates in comparative mythology didn't make first-class candidates for upwardly mobile businesses no matter how hard the little woman pushed. As for Arthur, he just went along, hoping things would work out.

They hadn't been getting along too well lately. The payoff came not long after Leafie's arrival, when Mimi dropped over unexpectedly one day with a copy of the latest best-seller, an autographed copy of *How to Succeed in Business Beyond Your Wildest Dreams Even If You Don't Want To!* which she had picked up for Arthur at the mall's B. Dalton, finding it on the "Gotta Have!" shelf.

Arthur came to the front door, but, uncharacteristically, didn't ask her in. Mimi noted this, and although she hadn't planned on setting foot in Arthur's house, thus avoiding his spasmodic amorous lunges which always messed her makeup, the fact that he was not asking her in this time struck her as deeply suspicious.

"Aren't you going to ask me in?" Mimi asked, with that directness that Arthur had found so enchanting back in the early days of their acquaintance.

"It's just that I've got some house guests and the place is a mess," Arthur said, thus exciting her determination to see what he was *really* up to.

"I'd like a drink of water," Mimi said. "It's such a hot day."

"Wait right here and I'll bring you one," Arthur said, rushing back into the house and shutting the door in her face.

Mimi waited, fuming, until he came back with half a glass of lukewarm tap water. She sipped it daintily, handed the glass back to Arthur, and said, "Aren't I going to get to meet your friends?"

"They're not really my friends," said Arthur, who had a genius for lame excuses.

His parents should have instructed him better. But Arthur's father, a jovial medium-to-bigshot lawyer, and his flower-growing, horseback-riding wife had been mowed down five years ago, driving away from Orlando International airport where they had gone for a bridge convention. Their deaths were caused by an Uzi-toting juvenile in a cut-down Corvette who, noting the jaunty little brush in Mr. Fenn's Tyrolean hat, had mistaken him for a wealthy German tourist and moved in for the kill. The youngster's plea of mistaken identity at his subsequent trial wasn't quite good enough to save him from a twenty-year prison sentence with a very good chance of parole after five years.

"Not your friends? What are they, then?" Mimi asked.

"Well, acquaintances, really. Not even that, just people I owe a favor to. What do you say we meet tonight at Thank God It's Friday?"

Lame, halting, and guilty-sounding!

"Are you ashamed of me, Arthur?"

"No! How could you think that? It's just that—"

"Then take me in and introduce me," Mimi said.

Recognizing moral force majeure, Arthur capitulated. "If you insist," he said, with what would have been dignity in a more self-possessed man.

Mimi entered. The first thing she saw was Luuma sprawled out on the couch with half a raw chicken in one hand, a quart of beer in the other, a plate of salsa and chips balanced on her belly, watching daytime soaps on Arthur's television.

"Mimi, this is Luuma. Luuma—"

"Hi ya, babe," Luuma said, jumping to her feet with horrid energy and spilling chips and salsa all over the floor. She wiped her greasy hand on her skirt, which was a half bolt of velveteen cloth wrapped loosely around her huge and ex-crescent bulk, and stuck her hand out to Mimi.

Mimi looked at it as though it were a rotting and radio-active fish, gamely grasped the fingers and drew her hand away.

"Passing through town?" Mimi asked, in a game attempt at what passed for normal conversation in her circle.

"Naw, we're here to stay a while," Luuma said. In an ear-splitting voice, she called out, "Hey, Leafie, come out here and meet Arthur's sweetie."

Leafie came out of the bathroom wrapped in a towel too small to entirely conceal his gigantic male organ.

Polite conversation became difficult for Mimi, although Leafie was perfectly correct in his somewhat hectic and pompous style. But the finishing touch was when Yah came out of the back bedroom, dressed in a kilt of baby pigskins that he had obtained from a local butcher who had thought he wanted to cook and eat them, not wear them just as they were. What Yah had on, as a matter of fact, was perfectly correct attire for a god of infanticide; but it was the finishing touch for Mimi, who became instantly queasy at the sight of the black blood that bubbled from the loosely basted seams.

"Oh my God," she said, "I think I'm going to be sick."

Just then Rotte came bounding out of the back room.

"Can I eat it?" he asked eagerly.

Mimi left in a great hurry. The next day she sent Arthur back his engagement ring (which she had had appraised and found not worth keeping) and a frosty note breaking off their engagement.

CHAPTER 11

WHEN SAMMY CAME OVER TO ARTHUR'S HOUSE FOR A VISIT, his reaction to the gods was completely the reverse of Mimi's. She had found them hideously gross; he considered them amusingly earthy. Nor did he have any great difficulty accepting the idea that they were, in fact, gods.

"You're a deep one," Sammy said to Arthur, balancing a bottle of beer as he sat in the living room and talked with Leafie and Luuma while Arthur sat nearby on a straight chair, dying of embarrassment. "Who would've thought that mythology stuff would ever have a practical application?" Turning to Leafie he said, "No offense, but have you got any tricks? I understand gods can do lots of tricks."

"Tricks? Sure we got tricks," Leafie said. "Hey, Luuma, show Sammy here how you do the bird."

"Watch this," Luuma said. She stood up, took a deep breath, and began to flap her arms. Faster and faster she flapped. She started to twirl, moving with amazing grace for so gross a creature. Soon she was spinning like a top, going impossibly fast, her red-and-black clothing (which Arthur had bought for her at a tent sale) billowing and flapping in the wind. And then she *really* put on speed, spinning so fast that she created a wind that stirred a pile of newspapers stacked in a corner. Then she began to dwindle, and when she came to a stop, she was transformed into a large raven with a red-and-black kerchief tied around her throat.

"Like it?" she said, in a sound between a croak and a twitter.

"That's great!" Sammy said. "Wow, what an act!"

The raven flapped its wings, began to fly around the room in dizzying circles, and then, hey, presto, she was Luuma again, slightly winded, but very pleased with herself.

"Wonderful, simply marvelous!" Sammy said. Turning to Arthur he said, "You really got yourself a moneymaker here, babe."

"As a matter of fact," Arthur said, "money is becoming something of a problem."

Sammy shrugged. "They should finish that investigation any week now and I'll be able to cut you a check. But you shouldn't have any money problems, not with honest-to-God gods in the house."

"Having gods as house guests costs money," Arthur said.

"Hey, we do our part," Leafie protested. "What about that stuff we brought in from Godsrealm?"

"The bullion? We spent all that."

"What about the other stuff?"

"I didn't know what to do with it," Arthur said. "I don't run a knickknack shop."

"Could I have a look?" Sammy asked.

Leafie went into the garage and brought out a large cardboard carton filled with items the gods had brought in from wherever they came from. There were rings and brooches, pendants and earrings, statuettes, cups and goblets, figurines, bracelets, and other bric-a-brac. Sammy went through it piece by piece.

"You've got some valuable stuff here," he said after a

while. "This looks like gold, there's a lot of silver, and I'll bet some of these precious stones are real. And the workmanship is real fine."

"I wouldn't know what to do with it," Arthur said.

"I do," Sammy said. "I've got a guy could appraise the gem and metal value. Some of it looks real old. I got another guy could sell it on the specialty antique jewelry market."

"Wouldn't you need to show where it came from?" Arthur asked.

"I got another guy can provide provenances," Sammy said. He turned to Leafie. "Why don't you let me handle this for you? I'll get you top dollar and take a straight ten-percent commission after expenses. That's fair, isn't it?"

"Sounds good to me," Leafie said.

"It's a done deal then," Sammy said, shaking Leafie's hand.

"There's this other stuff, too," Luuma said.

"What stuff is that?" Sammy asked.

"Just some stuff we picked up around the neighborhood when we were foraging for food. They're in the back of the garage under a tarpaulin."

They all went to the garage, where Luuma had neatly stacked two thirty-inch television sets, still in their original packing cases, a fairly new electric lawnmower, and a drill press.

"Where'd you get all this?" Arthur demanded. "I never saw it before."

"We didn't think you'd want to know," Luuma said. "You're the spiritual type, and we respect that. But your friend here is a businessman."

"Too true I'm a businessman," Sammy said. "Give me a couple of days, I know some people who know some people who'll take this stuff off your hands and give you best buck."

"Sounds good to me," Luuma said, and Leafie nodded.

"This is unethical!" Arthur said.

They all looked at him like he was the last freak left on Earth.

"You can't judge gods by human standards," Sammy said.

"I like your friend," Leafie said.

"I'll come over tonight with a van. Great doing business with you guys."

And Sammy left, humming "Happy days are here again."

CHAPTER 12

SAMMY'S BUSINESS ABILITIES WERE A BOON FOR THE GODS, and a considerable surprise for Arthur. Before his eyes, Sammy changed from a small, scrawny junior stockbroker who was something of a joke among his friends to an important south Florida crime figure with contacts throughout the state. There was more and more stuff to sell as the days went by, and Sammy showed a great aptitude for getting rid of it all, and hiding his transactions in mazes of connections, some kept on paper in codes of his own devising, others held merely in his memory. He was an adept salesman of the bric-a-brac and costume jewelry of the gods. He found suppliers for their food needs, and kept everything sweet by making generous contributions to police charities. And of course he was making out very well from his ten percent plus his almost infinitely expandable expenses.

No one called him to account. The gods, as Leafie once said, were not bookkeepers. And Arthur was kept busy with a matter that came up unexpectedly and soon came to dominate his life during this period.

Sammy raised the matter one evening when he came over to show the latest gains and to discuss some further matters.

Arthur stayed in his back bedroom during this time, reading Boethius's *Consolation of Philosophy,* a subject on which he was feeling an increasing need.

Sammy poked his head into Arthur's room. "Could you come out for a minute, buddy? There's some stuff we'd like to discuss with you."

Arthur had drifted away from the center of events after Sammy came aboard. This suited him just fine. He disliked the gods, and wanted nothing more than for them all to go to wherever they came from and leave him alone. He had raised this point once or twice, but Leafie had been vague about his plans, referring to his "mission on Earth" and its need for completion.

Now Arthur walked into the living room. Sammy, Leafie, and Luuma were there, and Yah was in the kitchen fixing drinks.

"Arthur," Sammy said, "we'd like to schedule a photo session for you for tomorrow. Would ten o'clock in the morning be convenient?"

"What do you want my picture for?" Arthur asked. "You planning to put a hex on me?"

They all laughed heartily at this. "Nothing of the sort, old boy," Sammy said. With prosperity he had picked up a few Britishisms, which sounded odd in his high-pitched nasal voice. "The position is, you see, we're planning to incorporate as a religion and you'll be head of the operation."

Arthur stared at him. "Me?"

"Titular head, I mean," Sammy said. "Not to put too fine a point on it, we want you to be the messenger of our new religion."

Arthur stared at him. "What religion are we talking about?"

Leafie looked at Sammy. "Tell him."

"Leafie and I were discussing this earlier," Sammy said. "I think we have a catchy name. We're calling ourselves NAR-

WAG. It stands for 'The New and Awesome Religion of the Wonderful Ancient Gods.' Has a ring to it, no?"

"But what right do you have to start a new religion?" Arthur asked.

"You seem to forget," Leafie said. "Me and my friends are *gods*. We've got a right to have any religion we want, and a messenger, too."

"What am I supposed to do?"

"You're the messenger. The one who made it all happen. You just have to stand around and look good. And tell people about our religious practices."

"What religious practices does NARWAG follow?"

"We'll be working that out as we go along," Leafie said.

CHAPTER 13

NEW GODS BEGAN TO SHOW UP AT THE COTTAGE ON SEA Grape Lane, gods brought in by Leafie and his friends. These new gods were different looking from the first bunch. Some came in for a few days, looked the operation over, and, not finding it to their liking, went back again to wherever they had come from. But one permanent addition at this time was Gegoman, whom Leafie introduced as an environmental god.

Gegoman was tall, with good-looking brooding features. He said little, seemed to think a lot. Leafie introduced him to Arthur one day then retired to the garage to let the two talk.

Gegoman said, "I'm still trying to make up my mind whether or not to stay on this Earth of yours."

Gegoman explained that he was not a fixed-form god like Leafie and the others. Gods had different properties, due to different antecedents. The definitive book on gods and their qualities had yet to be written.

Gegoman had several forms, and he moved or morphed between them in a slow constant flow. Sometimes he was a man and sometimes she was a woman. Sometimes Gegoman was both and sometimes not quite either. Sometimes Gegoman took the form of a hermaphrodite, split down the middle as it were, half-man and half-woman, one protuberant breast and one flat one. Arthur assumed it was the same with Gegoman's nether parts, though these were not exposed to his gaze and he hoped they never would be. Sometimes Gegoman changed into animal and bird forms, and once he lay gasping on the living room carpeting as a large fish, until he remembered where he was and came back to himself. Gegoman was absentminded, vague but compelling, elusive, and more than a little frightening.

"He's not our usual sort of thing," Sammy explained, "but we've held a meeting and decided it would be a good idea to have a nature diety on board."

"I thought the Earth had its own presiding diety," Arthur said. "Gaia, I've heard her called."

"Oh, yes," Leafie said, "Gaia is a dear, but she's temperamental. Quite recently she decided she didn't like how mankind was treating her and abandoned Earth. They say she went to some place that would pay her more attention. I've tried to get her back, but she simply won't come."

"What about Demeter and Persephone? They're in that line of work, aren't they?"

Leafie shook his head. "You've noticed perhaps that we have no Greek or Roman gods here, in fact, none of the gods of the major religions. There's a reason for that. They look down on us, you see. Consider us Johnny-come-latelies. Most importantly, they refuse to recognize my leadership, my preeminence in sacred matters. I really can't work with gods who question my authority."

"Where does Gegoman come from?"

"His antecedents are a little in doubt. He claims Olmec and Quechuan ancestry. But he has no papers to prove it. Frankly, we don't know where he comes from. But he *is* a fullfledged god, and seems to be serious about the environment. And he's willing to work with us. Claims he's sick of hanging around Cthuluville with nothing to do. So I propose we offer him a short-term contract and see how it all works out. All in favor? Fine! Opposed? No opposition. Arthur, you didn't raise your hand for either option."

"I really have no opinion in the matter," Arthur said.

"That really doesn't show good spirit," Leafie said. "Can we have a moment alone for a chat after the meeting?"

Later, alone in Arthur's bedroom, Leafie said, "Arthur, I realize that all this has been difficult for you."

Arthur nodded but did not reply.

"You probably think I've cheated you, or at least taken advantage of you."

Arthur shrugged, but did not meet Leafie's eye.

"It was necessary," Leafie said. "What is unfair in your human eyes is but a necessity in my view. Your own myths and legends are filled with stories of gods cheating humans, promising one thing, giving another. I can assure you that it can't be helped. Dieties have different agendas from humans, and different imperatives."

"Thanks for telling me this," Arthur said. "But I don't feel any better."

CHAPTER 14

LEAFIE HAD TRAVELED A LOT LOOKING FOR OTHER GODS FOR his pantheon. He had found Shango in a lean-to in a tropical jungle in south Godsrealm, drunk, maudlin, and self-pitying on palm wine.

Shango had been snubbed at a recent reception for Greco-Roman dieties. Mars-Ares had stopped him at the door. "Where are you going, boy? We don't want your kind here."

Shango stomped off in a huff. Back at his jungle shack, he tore off the black evening clothes he had created especially for the occasion. Royally, monumentally drunk, he screamed insults at the whites and their stuck-up gods.

He had raged until he was exhausted. Then he collapsed into a deep sulk, a mood he could maintain indefinitely, and it was in this state that Leafie found him.

"Bubbie, what's the matter?" Leafie said in that friendly off-hand way he had that convinced the gullible that he was basically a friendly, open sort of diety.

"They dissed me," Shango said.

"Who did that to you?"

"Ares and that lot. Wouldn't let me into their reception. I'd like to show them a thing or two. Prejudice is unworthy of a god, don't you think?"

"I'm certain of it," Leafie said. "It is so unfair that I've decided to do something about it. I'm putting together a new
pantheon."

"What's that?" Shango asked suspiciously.

"A pantheon is a collectivity of dieties," Leafie said. "Mine
will be organized along strictly nonracial lines. How does that
sound?"

Shango shrugged. "What good's this pantheon thing of
yours? Gods don't work the Earth anymore."

"All that has changed."

"How come? You got a special dispensation from the High
Gods?"

"I've got something better. I've got a human being who
has the key."

"What key?"

"The big key. The all important key. The long-lost secret
key that lets a human talk to the gods, command them, bring
them down to Earth."

"Solomon's key?"

"That's the one."

"Yeah, I heard of that key," Shango said. "A man gets that
key, he be stronger than the gods. You don't want to mess
with that key stuff, bro."

"I know all that," Leafie said. "But I also know this man.
He's got the key, but the poor sap doesn't have a clue as to the
power it gives him."

"You shuckin' me or is this for real?"

"Trust me, would I lie to you? This human with the key, he
needed a favor, you dig? He didn't know that all he had to do
was command me. No, this guy asked me nice, and seeing
how matters stood, I made a deal with him."

"Tell me about it," Shango said.

"I told him I'd do his silly little favor, but only if he gave
me permission to come to the Earth and do as I pleased."

"He never agreed to that!" Shango said.

"He did," Leafie said. "Gave me the whole nine yards."

"How come a man smart enough to find the key could be dumb enough to make a deal like that with you?"

"Hey, it's unlikely, but it happened," Leafie said. "And now I'm the boss of a promising religious organization I call NARWAG, and I've got the guy working as my messenger."

Shango laughed, a high-pitched cackling giggle which sounded strange coming from his massive frame.

"So you the boss!"

"That's right. I the boss. And I'm asking you if you want to come work for me."

"Sounds good," Shango said. Then he remembered his suspicious nature and said, "But what's our deal?"

"We can work out the details later. But you'll be on the pantheon's executive board and have an equal vote with the other board members. Can't say fairer than that, can I?"

"Maybe not. What do you get?"

"I'm the CEO of NARWAG," Leafie said. "That's only fair. I met the man and made the deal, so I get the last word."

"Yeah, you got the power," Shango said. "But it still sounds good. Include me in."

"Welcome aboard," said Leafie.

CHAPTER 15

SAMMY HAD ARRANGED A PHOTO SHOOT FOR ARTHUR FOR THE next morning. The photographer was a short, plump Latino man with brown skin and a thin black mustache. He came in burdened with cameras, light meters, lighting fixtures, and extra film canisters. The living room on Sea Grape Lane was in turmoil as usual. Leafie was having his nails done by a very small female diety with bat wings he had picked up somewhere. She fluttered in the air like a very large humming bird and chattered all the time in an irritating high-pitched squeak. Luuma and Yah were sitting in the window seat having a swearing contest. Rotte was sitting cross-legged on the shag rug polishing his necklace of baby skulls with a chamois.

"I'm Gomez," the photographer said. "Hernandez told me to come here, said you got some photography work."

"You're right on time," Sammy said. "It's a little busy here in the living room. Let's go to Arthur's bedroom. It's the only quiet spot in the house."

They lugged all the equipment into Arthur's bedroom. Arthur got up from the bed, where he'd been reading Schlemmener's *A Compendium of Ancient and Curious Lore,* fifth in the series.

Sammy said to Gomez, "This is Dr. Arthur Fenn, the messenger of the gods, chief representative of NARWAG."

The photographer nodded. "I'm Gomez, Acme Photo. Pleased to meet you, Mr. Messenger. You want passport photos, right?"

"No," Sammy said, "we want publicity shots."

"What kind of publicity?"

"These'll be for our full-page ad in the *Miami Herald*. Also for the brochures we're printing up."

"Color or black-and-white?"

"Both. And he's gotta look good."

Gomez studied Arthur and shook his head. His expression said, "You give me this to work with and you expect good?" In actuality he said, "Okay, we do what we can."

Gomez set up lighting, studied the effect, rearranged his lamps, put in filters and gauze panels to soften the effect, tilted Arthur's head this way and that way. At last he got a setup he liked and started shooting very rapidly with a battered Nikon. He went through a couple of rolls of film, finally saying, "Okay, that's it. You pay me now? Hernandez said you pay on the spot."

"Mr. Hernandez was right," Sammy said, "I've got your money right here. But I'm going to offer you a sporting proposition. One possibility is, I give you three hundred dollars right now and that's it."

"That's not too bad for an hour's work, I can live with that. What's the other possibility?"

"The other is that we let you run a credit on each photo of Arthur that we publish. The credit will read 'Photo by Gomez.' "

"Plus how much money?"

"No money. Your choice is three hundred dollars or a photo credit."

Gomez thought for a moment, then asked, "The credit

line, how much you think it'll be worth in terms of new business?"

"If our group goes over as big as I think it will, your photo credit will be worth tens of thousands of dollars. You'll be the first photographer of the messenger of the gods."

Gomez's eyes narrowed in calculation. "If this cockamamie thing takes hold, it could be worth a lot. On the other hand, it could be worth nothing at all."

"Take your best shot," Sammy said, grinning and fanning out hundred-dollar bills.

Gomez must have figured out something momentous was happening here. He said, "I think your boy's a comer. And these gods you got around here are really too much. I'll take the photo credit." He thought a moment more. "As a matter of fact, I want to make you a counteroffer."

"So make."

"You give me a photo credit, like you said. But you also include my telephone number. Do this and I'll do all your photography free."

"That's a nice offer," Sammy said. "But I got to tell you, photographer of the gods is going to be a valuable perk. We're not just going to give it away for nothing. Tell you what, you can have ten photo sessions on the terms you suggested, and after that, if you still want to work for us, we'll talk about you paying us a fee."

"I never heard of no arrangement like that."

"Look at it this way," Sammy said. "Suppose you had an exclusive to photograph Michael Jackson."

Gomez nodded. "I see your point." He looked at Arthur. His eyes narrowed. "You figure this kid's going to be another Michael?"

"Better than that. Arthur is the founder of what is going to be the next great world religion. Arthur's going to be the biggest thing since Jesus Christ."

"Don't blaspheme," Gomez said, crossing himself. "But I'm betting with you. I think you people are on the way up."

Arthur wanted to go for a walk after the photo session, but Sammy had set up a clothing session for him, and soon he was knee-deep in tailors, with seamstresses hanging bolts of cloth on him, bending over him with their mouths full of pins, putting a tuck here and a fold there, and the tailors standing back with pursed lips and narrowed eyes to judge the result. The rich fabrics seemed to say, "You're really something special." They dressed him in silks and satins, gave him waistcoats embroidered with gold and silver thread, and put on his head little caps covered with many-colored beads. And then they brought him fur mantles, feathered cloaks, luxurious shirts and blouses, some with slashed sleeves, and wide belts of soft Russian leather, and embroidered slippers with turned-up toes. And Arthur looked at the result in a mirror and was pleased. He knew it was all absurd, of course; but isn't fashion always absurd? And who is to judge a messenger's apparel but another messenger, or a god?

It wasn't until evening that he had a chance to be alone in his bedroom, settled down with a book. This was always the best part of his day. Since the arrival of the gods, Arthur had been spending a lot of time studying his ancient books. There was comfort there. He'd always had a taste for the mysterious, the abstruse, the far out, and the just plain impossible. It was what had led him into mythography in the first place.

No sooner had he settled down with the wooden-covered key to Solomon's mysteries that Mr. Avodar had given him than there came a tapping at his door. Leafie came in.

"Didn't want to disturb you, but I just got back from Gods-realm and I thought you'd like this." He gave Arthur a fragile palm-leaf book with a plastic cover. It was *The Yellow Book of Thoth*. Arthur accepted it gratefully. He was in the enviable position in which the gods themselves brought him books of ancient mysteries.

An hour later, Luuma came by with *The Great Sacrifice Records of the Lumerian Askleps*. It was not an original, but a very good copy, the only one on Earth, stolen from the Gods-realm central library.

And then, after dinner, which Arthur ate in his room on a tray, Rotte breezed in with *Dictates of the Warring Overgods,* and Gegoman followed soon after with *The Gods' Own Book on Killing for Pleasure and Sacredness.*

These last two were all in languages Arthur couldn't read; but the gods were always happy to come by and translate from time to time.

CHAPTER 16

ARTHUR'S HOUSE WAS HOT, CROWDED, CHAOTIC, AND SMELLY. Sammy wanted to buy the house next door to gave them all a little room to spread into. Arthur hadn't even known the place was for sale.

"The Samuelsons haven't completely decided yet," Sammy said. "But I've made them an offer they can't refuse."

"But what are you going to buy it with? Not my money! I don't have any. I still haven't been paid for that gold mine thing."

"I'm not using your money," Sammy said. "I'm buying the house out of the last load of gold and precious stones the gods brought me."

"Is it enough?"

"It'll do until the tithes start pouring in."

"Tithes?"

"From our new converts."

"I didn't know we had any converts."

"The first load is due to arrive in half an hour. We've just got time to go next door and close the deal."

"What do you need me for?" Arthur asked.

"Come along and see how it's done."

They went next door and rang the bell. Josiah Samuelson came to the door, a portly, white-haired retired orthodontist.

"It's you again!" Samuelson said. "And this time you've brought Arthur. Hello, Arthur."

"Hello, Mr. Samuelson," Arthur said.

"So how's the missus?" Sammy asked.

"She's still got that skin thing. You never saw such sores. The only thing that eases her is soaking in a bathtub full of Vaseline."

"I'm very sorry to hear that," Sammy said. "You remember, I warned you last week that it was going around."

"You said something about a hex."

"Yes, it's the gods," Sammy said. "They put out hexes when they don't get their way. I've asked them not to, but you know how it is with gods."

"I've also been getting a toothache," Samuelson said. "But my dentist can't find a thing."

Sammy shook his head. "The tooth hex. I told Rotte not to do that. But he gets so frustrated."

"Why should a god get frustrated?"

"He's sick of sleeping with all the others gods in Arthur's little house. He wants a house of his own. All the gods do."

"So why don't you buy him one? There are plenty of places for sale around here."

"But they don't adjoin Arthur's property."

Samuelson shrugged elaborately. "So he'd have to walk a couple of blocks to see his friends."

"No, it's not that at all. The properties have to be together to form a single sacred enclosure. The *temenos*, we call it."

"You're trying to turn these two houses into like a shul?"

"These and several others, Mr. Samuelson. We have offers out for the property on the other side, and the one behind. We're sure we'll make a deal before the end of the week. Just as we're going to settle for your property right now."

"Your threatening me?" Samuelson asked.

"Not at all," Sammy said. "I'm just predicting that if you think you got *tsouris* now, wait until you see what the gods have planned for you next week. But we don't want that, so let's go inside and look at these papers over a glass of your wife's excellent Carmel wine."

"What the hell," Samuelson said, "we were planning to move to Miami Shores anyhow. This neighborhood is going to the dogs. No offense meant."

"And none taken," Sammy said, one hand on Samuelson's shoulder, gently propelling him inside, the other hand plucking papers from an inner jacket pocket.

Samuelson moved out three days later. Sammy decided to use his newly vacated house for training classes. He brought Arthur along for the first class.

The converts had been trucked in from the Dade County drunk tank. There were ten of them, seven men and three women, all somewhat the worse for wear. They had been paid ten dollars apiece to convert to NARWAG, and do some work for said organization, details to be settled later. They arranged themselves on the folding chairs Sammy had set up.

"Now listen up," Sammy said. "I picked you people because you all say you want to work but you can't get work. Right?"

"Oh, that's right," one man replied. "No one will hire us because we're drunks."

"I've got nothing against drunks," Sammy said. "You can stay drunks and still work for me."

"Stay drunks? You mean you're not trying to get us to stop?"

Sammy shook his head. "In this organization we encourage drinking on the job."

The new recruits brightened up immediately. Then one

of them perceived a problem. "But where do we get the drink?"

Sammy smiled. "Our organization will supply you with liquor. And a little pocket money, too."

The drunks looked at one another with gazes of wild surmise. This was a dream come true. A drunkard's dream! But where was the catch?

"What do we have to do to get all this, mister?"

"I'll expect you to bring in a minimum of two new converts a week."

"Even drunks?"

"Even corpses," Sammy said. "As long as they have valid voter registration cards. At this stage it's numbers that count."

The drunks nodded. They had tracked him so far. Now where was the booze?

But Sammy wasn't finished. "We'll also expect all of you to keep your own voter registration cards up to date and be prepared to vote when, where, and how we tell you."

The drunks thought that over for a while. They had just found the catch in this too-good-to-be-true offer. One of them said, "Isn't it against the law to buy or sell votes?"

"It's not against divine law," Sammy said.

The drunks nodded, relieved at having found a solution to this tricky question of conscience.

The first drunk said, "Hey, it's no problem for me. But if the cops hear about this, there'll be trouble."

"Don't worry about the cops. I'll keep them sweet."

"Who are we supposed to vote for?"

"You'll be told in plenty of time."

"And where are the drinks?"

"Come into the kitchen and help yourselves."

CHAPTER 17

WHEN MIMI BROKE OFF HER ENGAGEMENT TO ARTHUR, SHE had expected him to call her the next day and grovel in that endearing way he had and beg her to reconsider. She had planned to do that, after lecturing him on his behavior toward the world in general and her specifically. Arthur's self-improvement was one of her favorite topics, and she looked forward to the conversation very much. When the hours passed and Arthur didn't call, she was annoyed at first, then dismayed. It occurred to her that something was going on here quite outside her experience. Not knowing what to do next, she called Sammy.

Sammy took her out that evening to Thank God It's Friday to discuss the matter.

"Oh, Sammy," Mimi said as she sipped her Roy Rogers. "Those creatures are monstrous, simply monstrous. How could Arthur allow them in his house?"

"You need to understand," Sammy said, "there's a good reason behind their uncouth behavior."

"What could it be?"

"The monstrous," Sammy said, "is modern man's only way of approaching the sacred."

"Is it, really?"

Sammy nodded. "Our age is not a time for the meek figures of a long-established religiosity. That doesn't work anymore. The gods, the real gods, are creatures out of nightmares."

"I can hardly believe it," Mimi said.

"You saw them yourself."

"Yes, I did," Mimi said. "Oh, Sammy, they were so horrible."

"That's the new paradigm," Sammy said, with the complacency of a man who was right in the middle of it.

Mimi considered for a while. There was a buzz of conversation and a blur of music in the restaurant. People were sitting at tables with drinks in front of them, having fun. Mimi wanted to have fun, too. But she had never quite figured out how to go about it. Emotions were always at war within her. She dreaded what she wanted, wanted what she dreaded. She was a serious-minded person, and yet she wanted to be gay, light-hearted, frivolous. Arthur had seemed a good compromise. He was as sober as she, by no means a light-minded person. And yet, his profession, mythography, was odd, mysterious, maybe even a little dangerous. So she had thought back at the beginning of their relationship. She'd been impressed by those old books, those amulets and talismans that he collected. They had an aura about them of something ancient and unspeakable. Something quite serious but not quite nice. And that had excited her. It had even provided—though she would never admit it even to Sally Jean, her best friend—a sexual thrill.

I must be real bad, she'd thought, not without pride, to feel such a thing. But there it was, and she had found herself—not exactly fantasizing, but having little flashes of fantasy, brief, illicit forbidden glimpses of her as a priestess of some ancient and disreputable cult. She saw herself within a circle of shaggy-headed worshipers, leading them in an ecstatic dance, standing in front of a roaring bonfire, naked to the waist, with deep shadows outlining her small, well-shaped breasts, her long, dark hair around her shoulders in snaky

strands, her eyes glowing. . . . The drums pounded, shrill
flutes wailed, the worshipers grew more frenzied, their hands
reached out to her—and she cut it off right there. Such non-
sense! Such a bad turn-on. She struggled to get her attention
onto something Sammy was saying. It was something interesting.

"The time of those old cults is returning, Mimi," Sammy
was saying. "The major religions are all washed up. They can't
produce. But we can. We got real gods, Mimi! They may not
be nice, but they're real, and they get results. And they reward
their followers who serve them."

"Serve them?" Mimi said drowsily. "I can't imagine what
you mean." She waited for Sammy to explain, feeling that illicit sense of sexual pleasure.

"A lot of people will serve them by making sacrifices and
dancing," Sammy said. "There'll be more and more of that as
the gods become increasingly manifest."

"I suppose that would follow," Mimi said noncommittally.

"You've seen DeMille's *Ten Commandments,* haven't you?
It's revived at Christmastime every year."

"Yes, I've seen it," Mimi said. "Charlton Heston going up
the mountain to receive the sacred scrolls."

"That's not the part I was thinking of. Remember the
scene where the children of Israel are worshiping the golden
calf?"

"Oh, yes. It was sorta shocking."

"Maybe. But it was also sorta exciting, wasn't it?"

A flash from the movie superimposed on Mimi's fantasy.
"I could never do that!"

"You could be the priestess, leading it!" Sammy said.

She stared at him. Had he been reading her mind? Or was
that sort of fantasy not so unusual after all?

"Me?" she said, with a shaky little laugh. "You think I could
do something like that?"

"I know you could," Sammy said. "I've seen you dance,

Mimi. You have a wonderful sense of motion. And you've got the looks, the figure—everything. You could be a wonderful priestess."

She took a moment to phrase her next thought. "But those pagan priestesses did terrible things!"

Sammy, too, phrased his next thought with care. "If the gods really live, and if that's what they really want, how could it be terrible?"

She stared at him, wide-eyed, glowing.

"And the thing of it is," Sammy went on, "we're in on the ground floor of this. Anything's possible at this point when it's all getting started."

"We?"

"I'm in this at the very beginning. And you could be too, Mimi, if you wanted to."

"You're not actually suggesting . . . are you?"

Sammy looked at her intently. Her hands were trembling. Mimi had always known he was interested in her. But a scrawny junior stockbroker had never been her idea of anything much. Now, however, he seemed changed, charged with the power of those strange gods.

Sammy dropped a twenty dollar bill on the table. He stood up and held out his hand.

"It's too noisy in here. Let's go somewhere we can talk. I can see a tremendous future in this for you, Mimi. You could be really important in NARWAG."

She followed him out to the car. She didn't ask where they were going. She had the feeling that a new life was opening up for her. It was frightening. But it was very exciting.

PART 2

CHAPTER 18

Let's take a sidetrack here, which will turn out to be very meaningful indeed for our story.

While all of this was going on with Arthur, the universe was quietly going about its usual business. Then suddenly it felt a sharp pain in its insides. That was due to the signal Arthur had unwittingly set forth.

What signal, you ask? Know that when mortals contact Godsrealm, the universe registers the sheer unlikeliness of the event in the most obvious of ways, with pain.

The pain was a sign of possible sickness in the general setup of what things are and how they happen.

The universe had learned to listen to such signs.

In its self-protective way, the universe created a being to take care of the problem. It created Asturas, a High God whose sole task was to go forth and find out what had gone wrong, and to do something about it.

Just to be sure the job got done, the universe created twelve other dieties.

These were a second line of defense. If Asturas was unable to handle the problem, the other twelve dieties would have a go at it.

Asturas's birth took place in a realm quite apart from Gods-realm. This realm didn't even have a name, though some referred to it as the Dimension of Possibilities.

The Dimension of Possibilities created a world for Asturas: a farm, a farmhouse, lands, cows, and a wife, the beautiful Letia, who had not only been forordained for Asturas but had been brought to birth simultaneously with him to ensure he'd have her.

None of this gave Asturas a swelled head, however. He was born with the knowledge of what he had been born to do.

Because of this knowledge he paid little attention to the farm, the animals, or his wife. What he had to do was perform the task he had been born to perform; the task that would save the universe from the destruction initiated by Arthur's action in contacting Godsrealm.

That was the general idea. But first Asturas had to figure out what exactly he was to do specifically.

That took some thinking.

He told Letia not to wait dinner and went to the minaret in one corner of his farmhouse, a place for meditation. Here he settled down on his cushion, went one-pointed, and started meditating.

Through intense cerebration he soon learned a strategy to undo the universe-busting effects of Arthur's action.

He needed to visit the Weaver of Worlds.

With the Weaver's help, Asturas would be able to do what he had to do.

It all came to him in a flash. That was the great advantage of having your destiny preordained. You didn't have to spend a lot of time considering various possibilities.

He came down from the minaret and said good-bye to his wife.

"I need to go away and do some stuff," he told her.

"Will you be gone long?"

"Hard to say."

"What's it about?"

"I've got to repair the central myth that sustains the universe and all other life."

"But I thought we were going to create our very own myth."

"Of course we are. We'll get to it as soon as I'm back."

The beautiful dark-haired Letia was unhappy about his leaving before they had even become fully acquainted. Asturas told her he'd soon be back to create a myth with her, an entirely different myth from the one he was trying to fix now, a myth about him and her. She asked him to not be away too long. And so he went forth.

Asturas went winging through the darkness of the cosmos. He flew fast and hard, not stopping to fool around with the stars and planets scattered in his path like grains of diamond dust. He passed the Milky Way without even going in for a dip, passing it up for the sake of his mission.

After a while he came to a big funky old factory building. It was made of some leftover gray universal building blocks. It looked funny, just hanging there in space.

There was no sign above the door. Those who could find this place didn't need no stinkin' signs.

Asturas went in.

He found himself in a huge room. Most of it was taken up by a gigantic loom. Someone was weaving on this colossal structure. The warps and the woofs of the loom ran off in all directions, the lines glowed and glistened, criss-crossing and disappearing at either end to infinite space.

A voice said to Asturas, "Yes, can I help you?"

Looking down, Asturas saw a spider who was also a woman.

Asturas said, "Are you the Weaver of the Worlds?"

"I have the honor of being that individual," the spider said.

"I need to find a particular strand."

"Which strand do you need?"

"One that averts the impending destruction of the universe."

"I know the very one you want," the spider said. "That strand began to twitch a little while ago, and I said to myself, 'I'll just bet somebody's coming to put this strand into play.'"

"That's what I'm here for," Asturas said.

"Let me show you the strand."

The spider had many deft limbs. She plunged her multiplicity of hands into the infinite strands of the web. Her fingers plucked one out.

"This is what you're looking for. Here, take it in your hand."

Asturas did. He gave a little yank. From far away he heard a faint cry.

"What was that?" Asturas asked.

"That was Dexter," the spider replied. "He's the one the line is attached to. Metaphorically, of course, but no less operatively for all that."

"I'll just follow this, then," Asturas said. "Thanks a lot. Much obliged."

"Think nothing of it," the spider said, and went back to whatever it was she had been doing before Asturas came along.

CHAPTER 19

EDGAR ALLAN DEXTER, SOLE PROPRIETER OF DEXTER'S NU-minous Services, was sitting in his pine-paneled residence in Sweet Home, Oregon, and feeling complacent.

It isn't often that mortals get a chance to do the work that gods are supposed to do, but often can't be bothered with. Those mortals who can get to do the work of the gods know they are onto a good thing.

Edgar Allan Dexter was such a person. Many years ago he had been in the right place at the right time to do a visiting diety a favor, thus sparing the diety an embarrassment no less annoying for being momentary and insignificant. The grateful diety granted Dexter a favor. The favor Dexter asked for was a job in the in-between area that affects both gods and men; the area that pertains to human-divine relations. The diety invented a job in this area and Dexter found himself a sort of semidivine ombudsman.

The work itself was a synecure: Dexter got paid for doing practically nothing, human-divine relations being at an all-time low just then. With the job came semidivine status and the chance to lead several interesting lives simultaneously. It was a once-in-a-lifetime shot: being noticed by the divine is very much like being noticed by Hollywood.

One of Dexter's lives was in twentieth-century America, where he worked as an agent for god-human affairs. In another, he lived on the Barbary Coast in San Francisco in the nineteenth century and ran a famous gambling establishment. In a third, he was ambassador to Paris, serving during the White House administration of Thomas Jefferson.

In his twentieth-century life he was a happily married man, retired and living in Sweet Home, Oregon, where he grew roses.

By jumping around between his various lives, he was able to slow the aging process to a crawl.

He had no idea how the gods contrived to let him live simultaneously in the past and in the present. He thought it was a neat trick and he didn't ask unnecessary questions.

It had all gone nicely for Dexter, but he knew it was payback time when the tall godlike being walked into his study in Sweet Home.

Dexter called his wife on the intercom and asked her to bring bagels, lox, and cream cheese for their guest. He offered the god a chair and asked him if he'd care to have his feet washed.

"No thanks, that's old-style," Asturas said. "I'm here to talk with you about a little problem that's come up recently."

"Nothing I've done wrong, I hope," Dexter said.

"Let's talk about it and see," Asturas said. "I believe you received a phone call recently from a human named Arthur Fenn."

"I got a call from a human," Dexter said. "Can't say I remember his name."

"It was Arthur Fenn. He asked you for help."

"Yes, he did. And I turned him down."

"Too bad," Asturas said.

Dexter shrugged. "How was I to know he might be important?"

"You were too hasty, Dexter. You let this human blunder

out alone into Godsrealm with no representation, and there he made a very disadvantageous arrangement with an outlawed god named Leafie."

"I didn't know about that."

"Evidently not. But you should have. Did you ever think about reporting it to one of the tutelary dieties?"

"I figured it would take care of itself."

"You figured wrong. Unless taking care of itself includes destroying the universe."

"The universe? The whole thing?"

Asturas nodded grimly.

"It seems to me you might like to undo the damage your neglect has brought about. I'm asking you to participate in saving the universe that you have so thoughtlessly put into peril."

"I'll be happy to do whatever I can. It's my universe, too, after all. May I just ask what this Arthur has to do with the destruction of the universe?"

"No, you may not."

"Frankly, I don't see what I can do."

"If you get back in touch with Arthur, offer your assistance, something could come up to improve the situation."

"Is that a prophecy?"

"Call it a presentiment."

"I'll get on it right away."

Asturas turned to the door and started walking toward it.

Dexter said, "Hey! Aren't you even going to stay for the lox and bagels?"

"I have no time for schmoozing, Dexter. And neither do you."

CHAPTER 20

ASTURAS, FINISHED WITH DEXTER, TOOK OUT THE CELLULAR phone he had been born with, and punched in a number that was complex, irrational, and imaginary.

"Universe Assistance Headquarters, Monica speaking."

"Monica? I don't believe I know you."

"I'm from the slyphid secretarial pool, subbing for the regular operator."

"This is Asturas. What's up?"

"Up?"

"What is happening that is of danger to the universe?" Asturas said, spelling it out, wondering why they had to change personnel so frequently. You'd think, in a matter as important as the preservation of the universe, people wouldn't mind working overtime.

"Yes, sir. I have it right here. There is a universal danger scheme that involves Cupid."

"Cupid? You're sure it's Cupid?"

"That's what my report says, sir."

"All right. What else?"

"An individual called Arthur Fenn is indicated as the source of universal upset and upheaval. Something momentous is about to happen to him."

"And what is that?"

"Fenn is to be shot with Cupid's arrow, thus causing him to fall in love with the goddess Mellicent."

"Mellicent? I don't know any Mellicent."

"Just another anonymous goddess, sir. Quite pretty, in the way young goddesses are."

"Where is all this supposed to take place?"

"It will happen at Arthur's house on Earth, on the occasion of the party being thrown for him by the minor god Leafie."

"Does Leafie have anything to do with this?"

"Our reports don't indicate it."

"Okay. How long do I have to get there?"

"I'm afraid it's a matter of minutes, sir, until the shooting takes place. Two, to be precise. And thirty-five seconds."

"I'm off!" Asturas cried, and vanished.

The cellular phone sat for a long time in silence. Then, after that, it said, in a tentative voice, "Would someone please hang me up?"

Silence in the place of no distinguishable features. After a while, a sound: the sobbing of a divine cellular phone that nobody had had the common decency to hang up.

CHAPTER 21

IMMEDIATELY AFTER ASTURAS'S DEPARTURE, DEXTER WENT TO the god-man labor relations board. But the officials at the contracts department were out to lunch. They had been out for a considerable time. A matter of some centuries, in fact. Dexter realized this after an hour or so sitting in the gloomy waiting room. It was the cobwebs that finally tipped him off; and the ancient dust on the cobwebs.

Dexter went into the corridor to see if he could find anyone. The corridor, too, wad dusty and cobwebby. He walked down it a considerable distance—it stretched for miles—and after a while he came to a door marked CUSTODIAN. He knocked, and getting no answer, turned the knob, and finding the door unlocked, walked in.

Inside he found a small office with a comfortable-looking couch. Stretched out on that couch was an entity—it was impossible to tell at a glance whether it was a man or a god, or perhaps something else. The entity seemed to be of the masculine persuasion, was of medium height and had medium brown hair flecked with gray. Dexter coughed loudly. The being on the couch opened his eyes, blinked rapidly several times, and sat up hastily.

"Yes, sir. What can I do for you?"

"I'm looking for someone who works on the god-man labor relations board."

"Yes, sir. That's me. Hoelle is the name."

"Is that a man's name or a god's name?"

"Both. I am a god, however. Though not a very important one, I'm afraid."

"I'm an enhanced man," Dexter said. "I have rather more powers than your average man, but I'm not a god."

"Don't let it bother you."

"It doesn't."

"Good. Do you have a complaint?"

"I do," Dexter said. "It involves a client of mine who signed a contract with a god named Leafie."

He showed Hoelle a copy of the contract which he had obtained earlier from Universal Procurement Services. Hoelle scanned it and shook his head.

"Your client seems to have given away all his rights."

"That's my understanding, yes."

"A pity. Humans should exercise more care in these matters. They keep on thinking a god will be scrupulous just because he's a god."

"I agree."

"Your client has made a serious error. There's nothing I can do about it. The contract is valid."

"I didn't come here to ask you to change anything. I'm here for a ruling on a matter of common practice. My client invited this god to his house, and the god invited his friends. They all moved into my client's house, which is a small one. And now my client has no privacy whatsoever."

"Doesn't he have a room of his own?"

"Not one that's safe from intrusion. I need to meet with my client, and under the circumstances it's impossible."

"That is unconscionable," Hoelle said. "I'll write a note on official stationery to ensure your client's right to a room of his own and to complete control of who enters that room."

"That's good of you."

"No hay de qué," Hoelle said. "The rules are stacked against humans in this universe. We do what we can."

CHAPTER 22

IT WAS DURING THIS PERIOD THAT ARTHUR SUFFERED A CRISIS. It was perhaps to be expected, and it is only surprising that it hadn't come sooner. 101 Sea Grape Lane had changed in a matter of weeks from the refuge of a reclusive scholar into the booming and everexpanding headquarters of NARWAG, a cult that was catching on like wildfire. Arthur was constantly bothered by reporters, by tailors, by Sammy and his assistants, by the gods themselves. He began getting hysterical at increasingly frequent intervals, his appetite was off, sleep was a forgotten country, and he was having a lot of trouble holding it together, all the more so since he couldn't decide what "it" was.

There's no telling where all this might have led—Arthur wouldn't have been the first god-visited man to go catatonic or to be led away in hysterical fits, and that was what all this was leading toward. But the first change in the situation came quite unexpectedly.

Try though he might, Arthur could no longer conceal from himself how much matters were slipping out of his control.

And the trouble didn't end there. Leafie had been acting peculiar lately. Although everything seemed to be going his way, the god wasn't satisfied. He had become nervous and irascible, given to long, incoherent speeches. When he wasn't snapping at people, he was caught up in long, brooding silences.

He made Arthur very nervous. But the crux came one afternoon when Leafie came to the garage where Arthur was reading. The god slumped into a chair. His face was tense and his lips were tightly pursed.

"I'm not going to take it anymore," Leafie said after a while.

"Take what?" Arthur asked.

"The incredible criminal slowness of the human race. They don't seem to realize who I am."

"But people are joining your cause every day!" Arthur said.

"Not fast enough. Most of the human race doesn't know who I am and doesn't care."

"That'll change," Arthur said in what he hoped was a soothing voice.

"Damn right it'll change," Leafie said. "I'm going to make it change."

"What did you have in mind?" Arthur asked.

"Teach them a little gratitude," Leafie said, with a tight, evil smile. "Here they got a real live god in their midst and they're ignoring him. Well, let's see how they feel after the plague."

"Is there going to be a plague?"

"There sure as hell is," Leafie said. "I've been talking to Kalpaus, a Finnish plague god. He's up for a little action. He's delivering Oxpox 5. The skin falls off in sheets, the blood turns to sludge, the brain shrinks to the size of a walnut and then explodes. Let's see what the high and mighty human race thinks after they've got that to worry about."

Arthur felt a great terror, but he managed to control himself. He said, in an almost casual voice, "Why not give the humans a little more time? Your religion is about to hit big time. You wouldn't want to be out of worshipers at a time like that."

"You think they're really going to go for me?"

"I'm sure of it," Arthur said.

"Well, I'll give it a few days more," Leafie said. "If they haven't come around in significant numbers by then, we're going to shake things up." He laughed. "But don't worry. Kalpaus won't take *you*. You my prophet, baby."

And chuckling to himself, Leafie left the garage, in a good mood for the first time in days.

Arthur saw that he had to do something.

And there was only one thing he could do.

He didn't want to do it, but he figured he had to. This mess was his fault. If Leafie called up a plague, that was ultimately his fault, too. He had to do his damndest.

He had to go back to Godspace.

That evening, while the gods were engaged in a drinking contest—their favorite athletic event—Arthur once again conjured up the miniature telephone kiosk and telephoned again into the infinite.

The same operator answered.

"Look," Arthur said, "I need help and I need it bad."

This time the operator was cross. "I was told to tell you that you are not authorized to use the godline. You are hereby commanded to hang up and never use this line again."

Hang up? Never call again? His last chance was fading before his eyes!

The extremity of his situation made Arthur bold.

In a demanding voice he said, "Hey, wait a minute! Who said I don't have authorization? The fact that I can call at all is proof that I have authorization."

"Well, I don't know," the operator said.

"It's obvious," Arthur said. "When did you ever hear of an unauthorized human using the godline?"

"It's never happened before. It's supposed to be impossible. It *is* impossible!"

"So there you are. Put me through to Dexter's Numinous Service."

"But there's an order out against you—"

"And I'm here to tell you it's a mistake. Now put me through or I'll have to talk to your supervisor."

Arthur didn't know where he had found such firmness. And the wonderful thing was, it worked. The operator mumbled something he couldn't make out, and put him through.

"Dexter here."

"This is Arthur. I talked to you before. I must insist upon your help."

"I was just about to call you myself. Aren't they respecting your privacy?"

"The problem goes a lot deeper than my privacy. Dexter, these gods are playing hell with the Earth. I've got to do something."

"Can you come over here?"

"I'll stand close to the phone," Arthur said, "and you pull me through."

Already he was starting to learn a few of the ways of the gods.

It also was his real introduction to Godsrealm.

CHAPTER 23

GODSREALM IS BIG. VERY, VERY BIG. NO ONE KNOWS EXACTLY how big because the gods have never measured it. The gods don't measure things. Distance, after all, is really a measure of effort, and since gods can go where they want effortlessly, and, much of the time, instantaneously, why bother measuring?

Humans measure things. Because of this, the gods are wary of humans. They are wary but they are also fascinated, just as humans are toward gods.

From a god's point of view, humans are forever measuring things and stating them in units, all this according to the theories the gods just don't understand. Gods' minds don't work that way. The gods could never figure out what makes the mind of a Pythagoras, a Plato, or an Einstein work. "How can they think such things?" the gods say. "Distance is very long. Time is—different. But everyone knows that." And they shrug. That's a gods' answer to the eternal mysteries that mankind comes up with.

So no one has measured Godsrealm. The gods wouldn't let a human in to do it. It's big, though. Plenty big. It occupies an entire sphere of spacetime all by itself. That's *big*.

All of the gods who ever have been or ever will be are scattered around Godsrealm. At least, we suppose they're scat-

tered. Actually, they could all be in one part of it and the rest
of the place could be terra incognita. No one knows. The
gods don't use maps. They're not visual thinkers. If one god
wants to see another god, he has only to think of him and give
a slight push with his intentionality, and whammo, he's there.
When you can do that, you don't need a map.

And since gods can travel instantaneously, they don't
bother walking places, and they don't need cars or horses
either, though sometimes they keep the horses for mytholog-
ical reasons. Out of sentimentality, as it were.

Any way you look at it, there's plenty of room in Godsrealm.
Each god has his own home and doesn't have to be within sight
of any other god unless he wants to, which is seldom.

Each god makes his own climate, too. Gods never invented technology because they had magic. From a god's
point of view, technology is just inferior magic.

The gods are not much on exactitude in the human
sense. Another way of saying that is, the gods are big on vagueness.

The gods are born with knowledge already existing in
them, instinctively, as it were, like baby birds or kittens. So it's
hard to explain to a human exactly what the difference between a minor god and a major god is. Although the gods
pretty well understand it themselves.

One way of saying it is that major gods are just more than
minor gods. They're more powerful, they have more pres-
tige, more presence of mind, and definitely more hauteur.
But if you asked a god how some gods became major and others minor, he would have no answer for you. It just happens
that way, he'd say.

However it comes about, the High Gods have a distinct
realm within Godsrealm. They keep pretty much to their own
kind, as gods, men, and animals are likely to do in most circumstances.

Even the homes of the major gods are more major than

the homes of the minor gods. That is to say, bigger, more beautiful, more awe-inspiring. But no one can say why this is so, since any god can build a house of any size and get any interior decorator he wants. It just seems to be a quality of the major gods to have an air that's godlier than the less godly air of the minor gods.

In human terms, the realm of the gods is a topological nightmare. You can have the home of one god by a vast and resounding sea, and right next door to him, in real terms, whatever they are, might be a god living in vast and limitless deserts. And next door to that might be a god of the underground, whose underground somehow is above ground but nevertheless is underground. Go figure.

CHAPTER 24

DEXTER'S OFFICE WAS VERY BRIGHT. THE BRIGHTNESS EX-panded into a glowing globe. The glow was not of the gaudy brilliance the gods usually affected. It was a dark blue color, almost restful, and it was not bursting with the sort of corrus-cations the gods used to signal their entrance. This globe of blue light spun in place almost soberly, expanded in a rea-sonable fashion, and at last resolved into the figure of a medium-sized, somewhat portly, balding man in a brown business suit too heavy for the climate, holding an overstuffed briefcase and already mopping his brow.

"Hi, I'm Arthur," Arthur said. "Are you the god Dexter?"

"I'm not a god, I'm a man. As I said before, I'm a very en-hanced man, but a man all the same. Dexter's the name, Edgar Allan Dexter, but you can just call me Ed or Dexter, just as you please."

"I need help," Arthur said.

"I know," Dexter said. "Sorry about earlier. I've been thinking about your situation. What you really need is an agent."

"Fine, but where could I get one?"

"You're looking at one. I'm an authorized god-man agent. You need me because you have entered into an agreement with a diety without the precaution of any representation, without anyone who knows the rules of god-human relationships to look out for you, to tell you what to look out for, to take care of your interests. That's why you need an agent. You *want* an agent, or ought to want an agent, to give yourself a chance before these jumped-up minor gods with big-time ideas crap all over you."

"I see," Arthur said, his face twisting in an attempt to assimilate all this.

"We licensed god agents are granted special powers by the board. If we didn't have them, we'd never be able to do anything, gods being what they are. I've taken a look at the contract you made and I've got to tell you it doesn't look good."

"Where did you find the contract?"

"It's on file with the Customer Relations Board of the High Gods. It's pretty bad. But I've got an idea or two. Let me poke around, see what I can turn up. I'll be in touch again soon."

And Dexter phoned Arthur back to Earth.

PART 3

CHAPTER 25

BACK AT ASTURAS'S FARM, SHORTLY AFTER ASTURAS DEPARTED
to consult with the Weaver of Worlds, his brother, Ahriman,
was born.

His birth didn't take place in the messy manner in which
human babies are born. Creatures like Ahriman are born
whole and entire, with important knowledge about themselves and the universe already in place.

One moment he wasn't there, the next he was in the
courtyard, six feet tall, stark mother naked, and blinking in
the daylight for the first time.

Letia had been taking a big vase into the courtyard. She
was going to fill it with water and float rose petals in it. But
then Ahriman popped into existence before her very eyes.
She was so startled that she dropped the vase. It fell to the
flagstone floor, shattering into a thousand pieces.

"Who are you?" Letia asked.

"I am Ahriman," Ahriman said.

"I never heard of you."

"I am Asturas's brother."

"No one told me you were coming," Letia said.

"I didn't know it myself," Ahriman replied.

Ahriman thought Letia was beautiful and said so. Letia told him to get lost. Ahriman went off by himself to the back pasture, where the cows were grazing. He sat down on a rock and brooded.

Just born and he already had problems: the problems of the second-born.

He was jealous of Asturas, who, being first, was obviously destined to be an important figure in the affairs of the universe. Whereas he, Ahriman, was nothing, nada, zilch, an anomaly, a mistake, a purposeless epiphenomenon produced by chaos and chance.

Not only was he the second born, he also didn't know what he was supposed to do.

He only knew that he wanted an important cause to follow.

But what could that be?

He didn't want to serve mankind. He didn't care about the gods. He gave not a fig for the fate of the universe.

All he knew was, he didn't want to come in second in a race for two.

He needed to do something—but what could it be? He had a sense even then that any action he decided would be rotten, vile, unpleasant, evil-smelling, unsavory.

Still, he wanted to do it.

But what could it be?

He sat on his rock and thought. And after a while, a cow detached herself from the herd and approached him.

"Hello, cow," Ahriman said.

The cow eyed him coolly and went on with her grazing.

"I just want to talk to you," Ahriman said.

The cow looked at him suspiciously and began to move away.

"I speak your language!" Ahriman called out in Cowelese. "We could be friends."

The cow said, "I doubt that very much."

"You're obviously a special cow," Ahriman said. "Couldn't you give me a sign?"

"What sort of a sign?"

"Well, what about telling me what to do next?" He added hopefully, "Maybe it has something to do with Letia?"

"Forget that," the cow said. "You've got more important work to do than coming on to your brother's wife."

"I knew I had something important to do! But what is it?"

"Don't ask me," the cow said.

"Who should I ask?"

"Why not try the mysterious lady behind the little hill?"

Ahriman walked to the other side of the hill and there he saw a woman with vine leaves in her hair, gazing into a hand mirror.

"Hi," Ahriman said.

"Hello yourself," the woman said.

"You come here often?" Ahriman asked.

"This is the first time."

"Has that got something to do with me, huh?"

"Yes," she said.

"Who are you?"

"I am the personified projection of the universe to come."

"There's going to be a new universe?"

"Maybe not. Your brother is working to preserve the old universe, which has long outlived its usefulness but which refuses to pass away gracefully."

"Wow," Ahriman said. "This is big."

"Yes, it's very big."

"What can I do to help?"

"Let me just sum up the position," the woman said. "Here you are, looking for a cause to attach yourself to so you can gain strength through purpose and thereby overcome your brother's preeminence. Or do I have it wrong?"

"No, you're right on. Tell me what to do?"

"Know," she said, "that I am the spirit of something entirely new, a new principle, a new life, a new set of values. You can be a part of all that. If you do what I say, we can tag your brother with being part of the stuffy old order of things. That gives us some sympathy, and you certainly need some."

"I like what you're saying," Ahriman said.

"I like a man who knows what he likes. There is something you can do for me and for yourself. Are you ready for it?"

"Yes, I'm ready!"

"Without a lot of tedious questions?"

"No questions!"

"And no 'I'm not sures' or 'Don't you think it would be betters?' "

"None of those!"

"Very well. Here's the deal. There is a certain goddess named Mellicent who can play a crucial part in this story, with only a little backstage work required to set it up."

"I'll go to her at once!"

"Calm down, buster. That's not what's required at all. What you have to do is something more indirect, and therefore subtler, than approaching her without preparation."

"Okay, tell me what to do."

"First you must seek out the diety named Cupid . . . "

CHAPTER 26

AHRIMAN'S SEARCH FOR CUPID TOOK HIM TO ONE OF THE AL-
legorical regions of the universe. Here he found himself wandering in one of those propositionary spaces that the universe
produces from time to time to keep things complicated. This
space had been neatly furnished with a variety of shrubbery,
and a mountain in the distance. Light glowed on all sides
with an air of expectation. Ahriman knew that this was one of
those moments when something was going to happen. He
wished he knew what it was going to be, because then he
could formulate his response to it. But as usual, here he was
all unprepared, nothing in his mind but the root thought:
steal a march on his brother.

And then into the scene there entered a young man or
half-grown boy, walking.

Momentarily defeating his desire to feel sorry for himself, Ahriman focused his attention on the boy. This boy
glowed with the inner fire of a god, and he carried a bow in
his hand and over his shoulder was a quiver filled with arrows. Ahriman experienced a great emotion of relief because
he suddenly remembered: this was exactly what he had been
going to do: come forth upon this place and meet this boy.
And though he hadn't remembered it at the beginning, it

had come to pass anyway, and that gave him a feeling of gratitude for the unbending nature of things, which does not demand that we obsess constantly over what is to happen next, but merely put one foot in front of the other until something numinous takes place.

"You are Cupid!" Ahriman said to the boy.

"Why yes, I'm the most recent Cupid. But how did you know?" the boy replied.

Ahriman was about to tell the boy that all the Cupids were famous, but desisted, for fear of giving him a swelled head.

"I just made a lucky guess," Ahriman said. "Nice-looking bow and arrows you got there."

"Yes, they are nice, aren't they?" Cupid said. "I don't remember exactly how I got them, but they really are neat."

"I suppose you like shooting arrows?" Ahriman said.

"Yes, very much."

"So you wouldn't mind shooting at someone if I asked you to?"

"Not at all. It's fun. Tell me who you want me to shoot at and I'll gladly do it."

This was going rather too well, Ahriman reflected. Something was amiss here. He was solving his problem without difficulty. There had to be a rat somewhere.

He concentrated. It occurred to him to examine Cupid's arrows. They were fine, straight-looking arrows, but there was a sticky sort of sap on the arrowheads. Ahriman was careful not to touch them.

"What's this stuff?" Ahriman asked Cupid.

"That's gall," Cupid said. "When I shoot someone with it, he feels all the sadness for days that will no longer come again."

"But that's not what you're supposed to be shooting people full of!" Ahriman said.

"What, then?"

"Love, that's what! You're the god of love and your arrows are supposed to inflame people with the passion of love."

"First I ever heard of it," Cupid said.

"If you really want to see some interesting reactions, it might be a good idea to try shooting people with love rather than irritation."

"You mean tip them with a love potion instead of an irritation poison?" Cupid asked.

"Precisely. Love will achieve the same effect as gall, and yet instead of fearing it, people will go out of their way to be shot by one of your arrows."

"That sounds great," Cupid said. "I've been getting a bad press recently. I'd like it much better to be renowned for spreading happiness."

"Love'll do it," Ahriman said. "I ask only one favor, this for my part in pointing out this important truth. That you let me tell you who to shoot the first love arrow at and the precise time to shoot it. Would you agree to that?"

"Sure, no sweat," Cupid said. "Glad to do it for you. But where do I get this love stuff?"

"Don't *you* know?"

"I haven't a clue. They just told me to get in there and shoot poisoned arrows. Gall is easy to come by, but a potion of love is rare indeed."

"Wait right here," Ahriman said. "I'll see if I can't bring you some myself."

CHAPTER 27

HAVING THUS RASHLY BOUND HIMSELF, AHRIMAN WENT BACK to a more familiar space, one in which he could listen attentively to the voice behind the voice of the universe.

But no voice was heard, so finally he said, "Oh Voice, tell me something that I may better serve you. Where can I find some love potion?"

"Why, that's easy to solve," the voice said. "You must go to Arachne and take some from her."

"And where is this Arachne to be found?"

"She is at her place in the heavenly constellation Scorpio. She lurks there, and lures living creatures into her web."

"How does she do that?" Ahriman said. "Don't people know better than to follow Arachne's web?"

"Arachne is very cunning. The strands of her web are invisible to common senses. The only way one can know them is by their scent. For Arachne secretes the poison called love, and she rubs this on her web, even the farthest-flung tendril, and a creature coming upon that thread will follow the scent of love until he is caught in Arachne's web, at which point the goddess eats him."

"That is not a good outcome," Ahriman said.

"Not for the eatee, but it is for Arachne."

"Granted. But I'll need to safeguard myself before going after her love poison. Do you have any ideas?"

"You can solve this one yourself," the voice said, and dissipated into the faintest echo of an echo, and then was gone entirely.

Ahriman took thought and realized that there was only one way of safeguarding himself, and it was a way open only to gods.

There and then, on the spot, and with no shilly-shallying, he split himself in two. The part which contained the part of him that did the splitting he called Ahriman 1. The other part, the part he split off, he called Ahriman 2.

"Now listen carefully," Ahriman 1 said to Ahriman 2. "I need to send you on an errand. But first I need to make sure that we both understand the position. I am the preeminent one. Agreed?"

"I suppose so," Ahriman 2 said. "I am perfectly aware that the you who is speaking to me created me from himself, and therefore I come second, though I don't have to like it."

"You don't have to like it," Ahriman 1 said. "You just have to accept it. So that much understood, I want you to proceed at all speed to the constellation Scorpio, where you will find the goddess Arachne, the great spider."

"Yeah, okay, I got it. I don't like it, but I got it. What am I supposed to do then?"

"Somewhere in her web you will find a container of love poison. That is what Arachne coats her web with, which makes her so fatally attractive."

"Yeah, okay, go on."

"You are to steal that container of love poison and bring it back to me."

"Okay, sure, I got it, no problem, what's the big deal?"

"The big deal comes," Ahriman 1 said, "when you find yourself in love with Arachne and therefore unwilling to leave her, even though you also know that when Arachne grabs you, she eats you."

"Hell, I'm not going to hang around for that. What do you take me for?"

"A creature whose life and actions are determined by love."

"Oh," said Ahriman 2, deflated.

"While you are doing this, I will be waiting here in this safe place. And I will command you to return to me. And you will obey me."

"Well, sure, of course I'll obey you. You think I want to hang around and be eaten? We're together on this one. As a matter of fact, you probably didn't have to split yourself in two at all to accomplish this. You could have done it all by yourself."

"I'm not so sure of that," Ahriman 1 said. "Now go and do what I've asked of you."

And Ahriman 2 departed at once for the constellation Scorpio.

CHAPTER 28

IT WAS A LONG AND DIFFICULT TRIP TO THE CONSTELLATION Scorpio. And it was dangerous, too, and afforded an opportunity for heroic deeds. But Ahriman 2 was in a hurry and had no time to waste on exploits. That would have to come later. This was just something to do, not to get famous from.

Accordingly, he chose to bargain with the threatening entities he met along the way rather than engaging them in combat. To each he promised to arrange things the way they liked them as soon as his predominance over his brother was recognized sufficiently to permit the development of a new world order.

To the Nemean lion he promised a huge territory in central Africa, his to have and to hold for as long as water dripped or fire singed.

To Procrustes, the celebrated stretcher of travelers, he promised a kingdom of his very own, and to the Midgard serpent he promised to produce a new green world around which the serpent could wrap himself.

He was not entirely sure how he would keep these pledges, but at least the granting of them had speeded his progress. So it was hardly any time at all before he found himself at the constellation Scorpio. And then it was but the work of a minute to locate Arachne's web in the upper-right quadrant.

The web had a shiny glow and was made up of many colors. Heavy strands anchored it to large rocks and short, robust trees. The web stood high in the air attached to the upright horns of Dionysus's lyre.

"Okay, I'm here," Ahriman 2 said.

His message was immediately received by Ahriman 1, who had been waiting for it.

"You're doing just fine," Ahriman 1 said. "Do you see where the love stuff is stored?"

Ahriman 2 narrowed his eyes and scanned the web with strong vision.

"Yes, it must be that brownish thing like a briefcase that's nestled near the center of the web."

"Sounds like that's it, all right. Now, where is Arachne herself?"

"I see her off in the scrubby little woods near where one corner of the web is anchored. She appears to be taking a nap."

"That is excellent. You can take this opportunity of stealing into her web and taking that briefcase."

"I'm on the case," Ahriman 2 said, and stepped lightly onto the nearest strand of the web.

Poised there, he looked over to Arachne. She appeared to slumber still, her noisome stomach full of the hopes and fears of her most recent meal.

Ahriman 2 moved lightly up the strands, which were sticky with the attractive substance Arachne had coated them with. As he proceeded, Ahriman 2 came all insensibly under the influence of Arachne's love potion.

He reasoned to himself, "She's actually very cute, that Arachne lady. I could go for her big time. She's misunderstood, I'm sure of that. Boy, wouldn't it be a wonderful thing to get together with that there Arachne in the passionate embrace that passes all understanding, the embrace whose life is death."

Although these events were taking place in his mentation, they did not stop him from moving up and up the strand, and into the web itself. There, moving more lightly than a human man could, he glided with light quick steps toward the center of the net where the briefcase full of love poison was situated.

He did not fail to note that it was an almost perfect afternoon, there in Arachne's web, one of those lustrous days that seem just built for lovers.

At last he was in the corner of the web where the briefcase was hung from a strand. Ahriman 2 plucked it loose and turned to back away from the web. He saw, as from a great distance, Arachne, just awakened from her slumber, proceeding at a leisurely pace to return to her web. She seemed not to have seen him yet.

"That's good," Ahriman 1, who had been clocking these proceedings from afar opined. "You've got enough time to get out by by the rear entrance before Arachne comes upon you. Do make haste."

"Haste is not necessary," Ahriman 2 said.

"And why not?"

"I have decided to stay here and await Arachne's return."

"Why would you want to do that?"

"Because I love her, Ahriman 1, love her beyond reason and beyond my hopes for life itself."

"That's wonderful," Ahriman 1 said. "But if she catches you, she'll eat you."

"I have been contemplating that fact."

"And?"

"And it seems to me there are two likely outcomes here."

"And they are?"

"I can convince her by my words that my love for her is special, new, unprecedented. And that she will be so moved by my declaration that she will desist from eating me but will live with me instead in a state of connubial bliss."

"And the other?"

"That she will eat me. But I'm not worried about that."

"Because you feel it is unlikely?"

"No, because I feel it is desirable. For what great mark of favor could a lover give to the object of his desire than that she should consume him entirely all on a summer's day?"

"I've heard enough," Ahriman 1 said. "Now hear this. You will promptly turn and get the hell of of there by the back door and you will do this immediately."

"No, sorry."

"What?"

"I no longer recognize your right to order me around. I hereby declare myself a fully independent organism, and I demand my right to make up my own mind about matters of import."

"Get out of that web! That's an order."

"No! That's a defiance!"

"We shall see," Ahriman 1 said, and he made a muscular movement and another entity appeared who had not been there before.

"Who are you?" Ahriman 2 asked.

"I am the judge of the urgency of the moment," the entity said. "I have been generated by the contretemps that exists between you and your other self."

"I do not recognize your authority."

"But you shall abide by it, nonetheless. By the power vested in me by both halves of the Ahriman personality, I declare that the credit lies with Number 1. So therefore, Number 2, obey your brother's mandate and get the hell out of there."

"I'll do it," Ahriman 2 said, "but believe me, you haven't heard the last of this."

He proceeded to the exit, arriving there just as Arachne

came upon the scene. She made a lunge for him, but Ahriman 2 jumped out of the way, and then he was through the exit and Ahriman 1, in his safe place, gathered Ahriman 2 back unto himself.

But though the personality of Ahriman was healed, evidence of the split remained, and in one part of his personality the seeds of revolt against his dominant half had been planted. This could be repressed for the time being, but would perforce come out later in response to the dictum, "Hidden or repressed contents must out."

But that was later. Right now, Ahriman had the precious poison of love and he wasted no time returning to Cupid. Cupid immediately coated his arrowheads with the stuff, but he didn't bother cleaning off the gall, figuring a little irritation would be no detriment to love and might even make it better, especially if you were a sensation head.

Now it was time for Ahriman to arrange the meeting between Mellicent and Arthur, a witness to which would be Cupid with his bow and arrows. To do this, Ahriman had to return to Godsrealm, where the fair goddess lived.

CHAPTER 29

THE MELLICENT WHOM AHRIMAN SOUGHT TO ENSLARE IN love was a goddess of the ancient pre-Islamic Syrians. Although her family were very minor gods, they were proud of their antiquity. Her father, Simus, was a former war god of a confederation of desert tribes. He was proud of his record as their commander in chief. It broke his heart when he was superceded by a newer god, but he maintained a stiff upper lip.

"They had a right to change their allegiance," he always said. But the family knew how badly he felt when the Syrians unceremoniously threw him out of office.

In a trunk in the back of his palace he still kept the ceremonial purple robe, the gold and ivory crown, the scepter of power, that had been his when he was in charge.

"We could have been very big," he always told people. "I don't think I'm exaggerating when I say I was the best strategist the ancient world has ever seen. Even in the best of times I only had a few thousand troops. The Syrians were never really fertile. That might have been your fault, mother."

This to his wife, Margaret, who had been a Syrian fertility goddess back in the days when he was god of war.

"I encouraged them to be fruitful and multiply," Margaret said. "But they always had a lot of other things on their minds. Too clever by half, that's what they were. And anyhow, the surrounding tribes were bigger. We got outbred, that's all that happened."

"Your idea about them impregnating all the women our people captured was sound enough," Simus said, "but we never captured enough women, and the impregnations didn't always take."

"And whose fault was that?" Margaret asked. "My warriors were virile, extremely virile. Trouble was, they picked up that Greek homosexuality thing. You should have never let them visit Athens."

"How was I to know they'd pick up the worst part of Athenian culture? Come back home with perfume in their beards and kohl on their eyes!"

"That did them no harm," Margaret said. "The real problem sprang from your habit of keeping all the young men confined to barracks, and not allowing them to see women until their thirty-fifth year."

"I didn't want to soften them," Simus said. "It worked for the Spartans."

"The Spartans never did have much population," Margaret pointed out. "Sure, they were good, man for man, and maybe one Spartan was worth ten of the enemy, as your troops were at their best. But what about one man against twenty? Or fifty? Or a hundred? Those were the odds you faced, my love, and there was nothing that could be done about it. Demography did you in, not spirit."

And so the talk went on, and they grumbled at each other, but for the most part lived together amicably. This was the sort of home Mellicent grew up in. There was conflict from the start about what career she was to follow. Father wanted her to be a war goddess, like Athene, whom he had always admired. Mother was dead set against it. "This warfare thing is not natural for a woman, and don't keep on quoting the Greeks to me. What are they now? A tiny Balkan country drowned in *bazouki* music, that's what they are now. No, my daughter will be a fertility goddess, like her mother."

But Mellicent didn't want either role. She liked the idea of herself as a love goddess, and it was in that that she had trained.

She didn't get much help from her parents. Both of them felt that love goddesses were a disreputable bunch, and anyhow, the whole thing was futile, for there was no employment for any goddess of any sort. The Earth had outgrown that sort of thing, except for a few primitive tribes who were being proselytized daily by Seventh Day Adventists and would soon succumb to the potent spell of monotheism manqué.

"I don't see why everyone is so taken up with this monotheism idea," Father grumbled. "These humans act like it's something really important. Whereas actually it's just as old-fashioned as polytheism. Akhnaton tried it and it didn't work. It hasn't worked for anyone. I don't see why humans keep after it."

"These fads have a way of catching on," Mother said. "Maybe in time they'll outgrow it."

"I hope so," Father said. "I'm getting too tired for all this."

Mellicent grew up in this household, isolated from other young gods and goddesses, for her parents were snobs and wouldn't mingle with people whose pedigree was less than theirs.

Mellicent and her family kept to themselves and never had much to do with their relatives. These relatives had for the most part been primitive nature dieties, and they hadn't aged well. Had grown quite senile, in fact, and now most of them were lodged in one of the numerous old gods' homes that dotted Godsrealm.

This was all Mellicent knew about the family until one day a handsome young god came to call. He said his name was Ahriman and that he and she were second cousins on his mother's side of the family.

CHAPTER 30

THE NEW GOD INSINUATED HIMSELF INTO THE GOOD GRACES of the household. Father liked him because Ahriman was happy to sit by the fire long into the evening and listen to Simus's descriptions of ancient wars he had fought. He was always respectful, eager to learn, deferential, and flattering. What could there be not to like?

And Margaret, more suspicious than her husband, was won over by the rave reviews this stranger gave to her raisin puddings, and the respect he paid to her beauty and lineage.

Yes, there seemed no doubt about it: this was a nice young god, and if a family were hoping to marry their daughter with advantage, one could do a lot worse than this trim and well-spoken young Ahriman. He even appeared to have serious intentions . . .

Oh, he never said anything about marriage, not directly, but parents understand about these things, and young goddesses, too. And so when Ahriman asked permission to take Mellicent to a special party on Earth, a party in celebration of a new human prophet, the parents were willing to give their approval, not that Mellicent really needed it.

And so it was off to Earth, the nice green-and-blue planet with all the white clouds. It had been many centuries since

Mellicent had last seen the place and it looked very good to her. She was wearing a classic tunic for the occasion, a pleated white linen, with one shoulder exposed—very Jackie O—and her hair piled on her head in a mass of curls, making her look like a young Artemis, actually better than a young Artemis because Artemis always was a snippy sort of person and it showed on her perfect young features. Too much pride by half: Artemis, of course, not Mellicent.

PART 4

CHAPTER 31

THE PARTY AT ARTHUR'S COTTAGE WAS IN FULL SWING BY THE
time Ahriman and Mellicent arrived. All the gods were drunk,
and acting more disgusting than usual, if that were possible.
Gegoman was roaring out an old war song and Shango was ac-
companying him on Arthur's bongos. Luuma had put on a
window shade and was prancing around with it in the firm be-
lief that this was the first time anyone had ever thought of
such a thing. Sammy was behind the bar, making drinks, with
the pleased look of a man who knows he's in on the ground
floor of what is going to be the biggest thing to hit Earth since
artificial illumination. There were a couple of local ladies
from the bars and taverns of Tahiti Beach, who evidently
thought that gods were almost as much fun as truck drivers.
The hi-fi was blasting the famous can can from Offenbach's
"Orpheus in the Underworld"—it was Leafie's favorite piece
of music with its unique combination of the classical and the
risqué.

Leafie, far gone in drunkenness, but still preeminent in
shrewdness, spotted the new arrivals as soon as they came
through the door, and went over to find out who they were.

"Hi," he said, "I'm Leafie, your host. But I don't remember inviting you."

"I'm Ahriman," Ahriman said. "And this is Mellicent. We're both gods—I'm a High God, actually—and we heard about this bash and thought we might drop in. But if we're not wanted—"

"Hey, I didn't mean anything like that!" Leafie said. "The more the merrier. I just like to know who walks in. I gotta watch out for my prophet, you know. He freaks when there are too many surprises."

"That's humans for you," said Ahriman. "By the way, where is he? I don't see anyone around here I'd take for a prophet."

"He's in his own bedroom, sulking," Leafie said. "He's a great prophet, but he can be such a pain, I can't tell you."

"We'd like to meet him," Ahriman said.

"Well, I don't know. He doesn't like me barging into his room with people."

"Hey, we're not people, we're friends," Ahriman said. "Aren't we, Mellicent?"

"I'm friendly," Mellicent said. "I'm studying to be a love diety."

"That's nice," Leafie said. "We already got one, but maybe I could get you on as an assistant."

"Hey, I wasn't looking for work," said Mellicent with a smile, "I was just making conversation, you know?"

"Come on, I'll see if Arthur'll see you." And Leafie led them through a painfully short corridor to the rear bedroom where Arthur lived.

Arthur was in his bedroom, reading one of his mythology books. Arthur had found that living with genuine mythical persons did not dispel his need to read about really mythical persons. It seemed to him that becoming real cheapened a god. Destroyed some of his mystery. Turned him into just one more self-server, albeit a powerful one.

And, as a human being, he found it painful to realize how

little the gods cared for you unless they lusted after your body. You only existed for them as a body, and they soon got through with yours and went on to the next. That was all very well for them. But what were you to do after a god or goddess has loved you?

These thoughts vanished from Arthur's mind when Mellicent came into the room. She was slender, beautiful, and gleaming with that special shine that heavenly creatures have, that luster, that lure, that gotta-have-it. But Arthur was not thinking of getting her for himself. Oh, the thought may have crossed his mind—he'd be scarcely human if it hadn't—but his low self-esteem quickly brought it to proper proportions. That's an exceptionally beautiful and desirable woman, he thought, and she probably thinks I'm nothing special, and she's right.

"Mellicent, this is Arthur," Leafie said.

She stepped forward and offered him her hand. The hand of a goddess! Arthur grasped the little fingers and felt the shock of her vibrancy, and all this while he was smelling her perfume and his mind and body were busy producing thousand of ergs of pheremones.

"Glad to meet you," Mellicent said.

"Delighted," Arthur said.

CHAPTER 32

ASTURAS ARRIVED AT THE PARTY AS CLOSE TO INSTANTA-
neously as makes no never mind. He had taken the precaution of making himself invisible. What he didn't need was
a lot of stupid chatter with Leafie and his friends. They
weren't in on the big scheme. They were interested only in self-
aggrandisement, not in saving the universe. They were con-
temptible, as gods serving minor purposes always were. And
even if they weren't, Asturas wasn't there for a lot of gabble.

Invisible, Asturas slid past Ahriman and glided through
the crowded noisy party. For him it was like an affair of ghosts,
soundless, impalpable. He moved along, searching for Cupid.
But just then Arthur and Mellicent came out of Arthur's bedroom.

So this rather nondescript human was the cause of all this
turmoil! It seemed hardly possible, looking at the man with
his unprepossessing features. But that's how it happened
sometimes.

There was Cupid, ducked down behind a potted palm.
Cupid was invisible also, at least to the minor gods and humans assembled there. But you can't hide from the High
Gods, and Asturas saw him easily enough: a rather plump little boy with curly hair and a bow and arrows.

Asturas moved forward, thinking to become visible and argue the situation with Cupid. But he saw at once that that wouldn't help. The little godling was below the age of reason, just doing things on the impulse of the moment. For him, this thing was a lark. He would not be easily dissuaded of it.

So Asturas decided upon a different tactic. He waited until the last moment, when Cupid had taken aim.

Then, just before the winged godling could release his arrow, Asturas jostled Cupid's elbow.

The arrow flew . . .

CHAPTER 33

ASTURAS HAD DONE WHAT HE COULD. NOT BOTHERING TO check the results, he returned home. He had been thinking about what myth to enact with his wife, Letia. He had in mind something grandly romantic, yet with classical overtones. He was so busy thinking about what myth to go for, and exactly how he was going to create it, that it took him a while to realize the farm was deserted.

He rushed out to ask the cows. "Did you see my wife Letia leave?" They said no, but they were strangely evasive. It was as if they knew something but didn't want to tell him. Asturas didn't know why this should be, but thought it was the cow's well-known resistance to being turned into roast beef, which is the usual fate for a cow with bad news.

He returned to the bedroom and went into intensive deduction mode. It didn't take him long to realize that Letia had packed no luggage. All her clothes were there. There was no message for him . . . nothing except, now that he looked more closely, two letters scratched in the dust of the tiled floor.

The letters N. I.

What could they mean?

A quick search through his capacious memory convinced

the god he didn't know what Letia meant by those two cryptic letters. Who could tell him what they meant? He realized he must avail himself of a human oracle. Humans were clever about such things.

There was no time to lose. He ran to the end table in the next room, picked up the God Services Directory beside the godphone, and looked up Oracles, Human. The directory's pages fluttered open. Asturas called on the small built-in genie of the directory for assistance. He scanned the page, waiting for a sign. One came—his gaze, involuntarily, as it were, lingered on a name. A Señor Juan García, a circus performer, working out of Chichicalco in the mountains of Guerrero.

Asturas went there. On the outskirts of Chichicalco, he found the circus: a bunch of old trucks with circus gear piled high on them. They were beginning to set up in the fairground north of the city itself.

Asturas had taken on the disguise of an entrepreneur from Ringling Brothers and Barnum and Bailey. He found García off to one side, giving unneeded advice in the setting up of the main tent.

García saw through him at once. "You're a god?"

"A High God," Asturas said.

"Then it's no use telling you to come back later."

"No use at all. Talk to me now, oracle, or endure the fate that awaits one who keeps the High Gods waiting."

"All right, don't get angry. What did you want to see me about?"

"I received the initials N I in a context which was unmistakably meaningful. I need to know what they mean."

García laughed: a short, ugly bark of a sound. He grinned and fingered the dirty silk scarf knotted around his neck, unshaven face broad and brown-eyed.

"That is simple enough. N I refers to note inferential, a new designation by the Inferential post office."

"What is the Inferential post office? And why wasn't I told about it?"

"As for your not being told about it; have you checked your mail recently?"

"I've been busy," Asturas said.

"They can't notify you about a new mail service unless you read your mail."

"Thanks a lot. Now tell me what a note inferential is."

"A note inferential is a message that someone leaves you when he or she or it doesn't have enough time to produce a regular note. This is a new service some of your fellow gods have put together to expedite communication; for sometimes events move too fast for any other means of communication."

"This note to me is to be found in the Central God post office, I imagine?"

"You imagine correctly," García said. "The charge for my service will be three gold pieces. I know you were just about to ask."

Asturas paid and hurried away. He flew up into space, and then moved into the space between spaces, the crawlspace of the godly domains. In this interspace he made good time, and came at last to that lordly square at the end of a mighty concourse where the Post Office of the Gods, with its Corinthian columns and gleaming Parian marble facing, existed as a wonder to all the worlds.

Hurrying inside, Asturas noted there was a new window. Written on top of it were the words CALL HERE FOR INFERENTIAL NOTES.

Asturas walked up to the counter, and, pounding on the counter to get someone's attention, he called for his note. The clerk looked a bit surly at being called so preemptorily, but, noting that Asturas was a High God, this evident from the reddish glow of his halo, put aside chiding words and quickly brought the god what he sought.

Asturas retired to a little cafe near the post office, and

there, over a cup of ambrosial coffee, he opened the note. It was from Letia. And it was thirty pages long.

Inferential notes tend to go on and on. This one certainly did. But at last Asturas got to the meaty part:

> I don't think you know this, but shortly after you left your brother was born. His name is Ahriman and he's a nasty bit of work. He made advances on me which I repulsed with indignation. After that, he took to hanging around with the cows. They must have told him something. I always told you the cows knew more than you'd think, but you never listened to me. After talking to them, Ahriman went off, grinning and pleased with himself. To make your life a hell, so I think. Later he came back, and he looked pleased as punch. "And now," he said, "for the unfinished business between you and me." I knew at once what he meant. I was a defenseless female goddess, and I had no means of escape. He left me only enough time to intend this inferential note to you. I only hope you know about the Inferential Postal Service. It was announced in the mail but you were away. Otherwise, you won't know what to do. And our legend, which I look forward to very much, will never get created.
> Your loving wife, Letia.

Asturas ground his teeth, but that did no good. He needed to find out where Ahriman had taken Letia. Luckily, the inferential note had an inferential forwarding address: The Caves of Lethe.

CHAPTER 34

THE CAVES OF LETHE WAS A RESORT HOTEL IN ONE OF THE newer sections of the underworld. Outside the main hotel, in the sculptured grounds, there were a number of tiled swimming pools. Water bubbled up into them from underground sources.

There were a lot of guests today. Barbarossa and his warriors were there, granted a day holiday from their cavern somewhere in the Teutonic Alps. They were disporting in the waters of dream within a dream. Soon they would have to return to their cave and await their real awakening.

The seven sleepers of Ephesus were here, having cocktails in deck chairs.

The kraken, relived for a little while of his eternal task of sleeping in the limitless depths of ocean in front of the blueblack walls of Atlantis, was sporting in a pool with dolphin maidens, enjoying his brief holiday.

"Nice to see everyone's having fun," Asturas said to the guide who had been assigned to him.

"All famous sleepers are accorded brief holidays from their work of forgetfulness. Is the one you want here?"

Asturas looked but did not see Letia among any of the people in the tiled pools.

"Then let us proceed a little farther," his guide said. "Over here is the Pool of Dreams, fed by the veritable oneiric current. Here is the Wading Pool of Delightful Anticipation, where a person doesn't know if he is awake or asleep, but drifts in a state halfway between the two, sometimes descending toward oceanic consciousness, sometimes descending into valiant dreams."

This stream brought all the visions that had been ascribed to opium and its derivatives, but with no hangover and no aftereffects. And with no habituation, because the dreams and the fantasies stayed forever fresh.

"She's not here," Asturas said.

"Then she must be in the Lethe spa section proper. All who drink Lethe's waters become bereft of memory, and exist in an eternal floating now. It is a pleasant state, though one has little of one's previous capacity. Here men leave their unwilling women, quelling their rebelliousness with forgetfulness."

And it was there that he found her: lovely Letia, lounging on the side of a pool in a fetching bikini, her long hair flowing about her shoulders.

"Hello," Asturas said.

She smiled at him and returned to her fashion magazine. It was obvious she didn't know him.

Asturas's mind was filled with grief and he asked the attendant, "Is there nothing that can be done?"

"There is," the attendant said. "We have a special preparation for those who want their loved ones's memories restored. But many do not use it, because they often find their beloved more charming without memories, and therefore without a clue as to what to scold about, at least for a while."

Asturas insisted that such was not his case. He and Letia were newly wed, and it would be a while before he would have any complaints about her. So they brought in the antidote, which was given to Letia disguised as a frosted strawberry margarita, the drink that neither gods nor humans can resist. And in a trice, or slightly faster, Letia's memories were restored.

But it soon became apparent that something had gone wrong in the restoration process.

"Franklin!" she said. "Where's Franklin?"

"Who is Franklin?" Asturas asked.

"My husband, of course, and president of the United States."

The cruel truth was now revealed. Letia had been given an antidote concocted for somebody else. And now she was in possession of someone else's memories, which she believed were her own.

Further questioning revealed that she thought she was a mortal named Eleanor Roosevelt—a human of the female persuasion whom many humans had modeled themselves on. She kept on talking about some event, perhaps imaginary, called the Second World War.

Asturas could only get her to come with him by pretending to be a human named Wendell Wilkie, on whom Mrs. Roosevelt seemed to have a crush.

When he told Letia that he had to leave her again, she said, "It's all right, Wendell." She was used to the dislocations of high office.

PART 5

CHAPTER 35

BACK IN GODSREALM, THE GODS' MONTHLY FEAST WAS HELD in Clostermacher Hall, which occupied a central position in the godzone. It was a for-members-only affair, restricted to dieties, thus excluding the familiars, trolls, elementals, ghosts, ghouls, and other entities who tried to crash it from time to time.

The god Loki was just picking up the wassail bowl when he heard a knock at the door. He was the closest, so he answered it.

Standing at the door was someone Loki didn't recognize. "What do you want?"

"My name is Scabber," the new arrival said. "I just got here."

Loki shrugged. "So what do you want?"

"I'd like to join the feast," Scabber said. "I hear it's open to all gods."

Loki looked him over. Scabber was medium-sized for a god, and neither fat nor thin. He had a long face and was not too bad looking. He had crisp brownish-red hair that stood up on his head like a brush. That gave Loki an idea.

"Are you a fox god, by any chance? Maybe one of the Japanese or Chinese ones, or Ainu perhaps?"

Scabber shrugged. "Could be. Frankly, I have no idea."

"But you *are* a god?"

"Of course." And Scabber turned on his nimbus, the faint violet glow around his head and shoulders showed that he was immortal, the sine qua non for a god.

Loki hesitated. Unknown gods did show up in Godsrealm from time to time. Not every diety was famous. Among the gods, some were better known than others, and some were not known at all. Some seemed to have no background, no family or friends, no family tree or history, nothing except their godhood, such as it was.

"Just a moment, let me talk with the others," Loki said.

He went back inside and told the other gods about the conversation.

"Let him in," Hralmar said. "If he's a ringer, we'll find out soon enough." The others concurred.

Scabber entered and found a place at the long table of the gods. Most of them noticed that he had the nimbus of immortality, but nothing much besides that. He took no part in the conversation, didn't seem to have a totemic animal, bird, or insect, told no stories about "the good old days," when gods interacted freely with humans. When Earth was mentioned, he seemed to know next to nothing about it, and he was equally vague about everything else. The gods couldn't help but think, Where did this lunkhead come from?

Toward dessert and coffee, Athene, who was seated near him, tried to include the newcomer in the conversation. She said, "Tell us, Scabber, is there some amusing story connected with how you came into being? I, for example, was born from my father's forehead. What about you?"

Scabber looked blank. "Can't really say. One day I opened my eyes and there I was, lying under a tree in limbo, fully grown and formed, and even dressed in green and russet."

Athene tried again: "Did you find any objects nearby at the time of your birth, like sacred scarabs, amulets, or talismans?"

"Nope," Scabber said. "Just me. After a while I realized there had to be other gods around, so I looked around and came here."

The conversation languished. Soon after, the feast ended and the gods left, and Scabber wandering off as though he didn't know what to do next.

In conversation with Artemis later, Athene said, "Not a scintillating conversationalist, but at least this new god is straightforward."

Artemis wasn't so sure. "He's probably not clever enough to tell a convincing lie."

CHAPTER 36

SCABBER FOUND AN UNCLAIMED LOT IN A SMALL VALLEY IN Godsrealm and built a small home there. He gave it a temperate climate, but didn't bother with any other improvements.

Over the next few weeks, Scabber kept pretty much to himself. He seemed detached, apathetic.

Then Leafie returned from Earth to boast of his exploits and look for a few more recruits. Unexpectedly, Scabber was interested in what he had to say.

Scabber met Leafie by appointment in the Crystal Ship, a privately owned restaurant. There, in a paneled booth over a couple of godbrews, Leafie boasted of the sweet deal he had made with Arthur Fenn, the first human to contact Godsrealm in a very long time.

"I don't see anything so great in making a deal with a mortal," Scabber said. "Happens all the time."

"It used to," Scabber told him. "But it's been centuries since the last human got in touch."

"Didn't know that," Scabber said.

Leafie nodded. "People aren't interested in the gods anymore, what with the general trend on Earth toward Nothingism. We used to have a good business in granting wishes, but nowadays, human missionary groups have been vying successfully for human souls."

"How were you able to convince this human to let you do it?"

Leafie laughed. "Like taking candy from a cherub. This Arthur Fenn fellow invited me to Earth, and didn't know squat about the possible consequences. I was able to get an open-ended agreement from him. Me and my friends have access to Earth, and we can do pretty much as we please."

"Sounds good," Scabber said, but he was thinking how much he disliked Leafie's smirk and his clever-than-thou attitude.

"Way it is now," Leafie continued, "me and my buddies range about the Earth free as you please. I've set up a religion, and we're making converts right and left. It's the biggest shot any of us has had in centuries."

"Sounds pretty good," Scabber admitted.

"I have room for one or two more good gods or goddesses. But remember, I'm in charge. If you want in, you gotta swear loyalty to me."

"I'll let you know," Scabber said, finished his brew and left.

He went away thoughtful. He wanted something to do. But he couldn't see himself serving under Leafie. The god had no more stature than he had, but he was puffing himself up, acting like a High God instead of the miserable little unknown diety he was.

Did he want to work for this guy? Hell, no! But he'd like to see Earth. As for Leafie . . . he didn't like the fellow. Quite disliked him, in fact. The more he thought about it, the more Scabber realized he'd rather do Leafie a bad turn rather than a good one.

He was interested when, a day later, he saw a notice on the gods' bulletin board.

It read,

> Edgar Allan Dexter, licensed agent for transactions between gods and men, a human being of planet Earth, is looking for a few good gods who aren't afraid of a little fighting. They will be working in a good cause. Interested parties may contact me at the Limbo Inn in downtown Limbo.

Scabber went to the Limbo Inn and was granted an interview with Dexter.

Dexter had taken a sitting room on the second floor. Just a bare-bones place, a couple of chairs and a table. He was taking papers out of a briefcase when Scabber walked in. He waved Scabber to a chair.

Scabber said, "Who are you planning to fight?"

Dexter looked him over, then said, "You know about Leafie and his friends?"

"I do, and if this involves working with that bunch, I'm not interested."

"Sit down, have a glass of soma. This proposition is for a human named Arthur Fenn."

"That's the guy Leafie's been talking about."

"That's right."

"So you'd be working with Leafie?"

"Not at all. Quite to the contrary. I'm looking to give Leafie one in the eye. If you're a friend of his, I don't think you'd be interested."

Scabber poured himself a glass of soma from the pitcher on the table, took a swallow, and said, "I'm no friend of Leafie. What do you propose?"

Dexter said, "Leafie has taken advantage of my client, Arthur Fenn. Knowing nothing about god-human relations, Arthur let Leafie and his friends loose on Earth, and put himself at a terrible disadvantage. He made a very bad deal. However, nothing in his agreement with Leafie is exclusive. Nothing prevents Arthur or his representative from bringing in other gods if he so pleases."

"And why should he want to do that?"

"Because Arthur needs allies, and Leafie needs a comeuppance."

"You mean like getting thrown off Earth?"

"That was what I had in mind," Dexter said.

"What's in it for me?" Scabber asked.

"What I offer," Dexter said, "is a chance at some action and good fighting, and the possibility of becoming one of the dieties of Earth. Given your circumstances, I think you may agree that's considerable."

Scabber nodded. He was no bargainer, no cunning dealmaker, and this human obviously knew a thing or two about gods and entering into agreements with them. And he was right, it would be better to be in action than to sit around his house wondering what to do with himself. And he wasn't about to pass up a chance to do Leafie a bad turn.

"How long have I got to think it over?" he asked.

"I must have your answer right now," Dexter said.

Scabber said, "Yes, I will go to Earth, I will befriend this Arthur, and I will defeat the insufferable Leafie."

CHAPTER 37

SCABBER GOT HIS INSTRUCTIONS FROM DEXTER AND PRO-
ceeded to Earth. With the sketched map Dexter gave him, he
was able to find Florida without too much trouble, and then
he just had to follow A1A to Tahiti Beach.

Once there, he came out of invisibility and looked around.
He liked what he saw, especially the beach with its striped um-
brellas and the beach girls in candy colors. He could have
hung around and watched them all day. But there was important stuff to do.

He walked to the little cottage at 101 Sea Grape Lane to
pay his respects to Arthur.

As he walked up he saw a sign on the lawn. It read: NO VIS-
ITORS EXCEPT BY PREVIOUS INVITATION.

Sitting in a deck chair on the lawn was a tall slack-jawed
young human in cutoffs with a shotgun across his knees.

Not even a god likes to get hit with shotgun pellets.

Scabber walked on.

Arthur was guarded. Scabber hadn't considered that possibility. He needed to make some plans. Of course, Leafie and
his fellow gods weren't going to admit him to Arthur's presence. Not willingly.

There was a way, however. Dexter had obtained a court order to the effect that Arthur's bedroom was his own and inviolate. Scabber could meet Arthur there. But how was he to get in? He'd have to get permission from Arthur himself. But there was no immediate or obvious way to do that.

If a god has a problem, he goes to an oracle. Oracles speak in riddles to mortals, but they lay the matter out straight for gods. They better, as long as they know which side their manna is buttered on.

Scabber consulted his guide to oracles of Earth. The nearest was working a sideshow act in Chichicalco, Mexico. Scabber went there via godpower, arriving at the little village in the mountains of Guerrero just at sunset, an hour before the circus opened for business.

Scabber walked out to the edge of town where the circus was camped. Juan García, human oracle, was sitting on a plastic milk carton outside his tent eating a bowl of chilaquiles. He was not even startled when Scabber suddenly appeared in front of him, leaning negligently against the adobe wall and whittling on an agave cactus.

"So what do you want me to oracularize for you?"

"I am faced with the following situation—" Scabber began, but Juan García interrupted him.

"I've read it from your mind already. Look, what you need to do is write this guy Arthur a letter. Tell him you're there to help and ask him for an interview in his bedroom. If he assents, you'll know it and be able to project yourself directly into his bedroom without going through Leafie or any of the others."

"But what if Leafie opens the letter?"

"Mark it godtalk, privileged. It'll go straight to Arthur's night table."

"I like it," said Scabber. "I'll try your suggestion."

"That'll be ten pieces of gold."

"I'll have to pay you next time," Scabber said. "I came out without any money."

García made no comment. But he knew no luck would come to a god who didn't pay for his oracular reading.

CHAPTER 38

TWO DAYS LATER, ARTHUR WAS MORE THAN A LITTLE SUR-
prised when a letter appeared on his night table. It read:

> Dear Mr. Fenn,
>   My name is Scabber and I am a diety. Your
> agent, Mr. Dexter, told me about your case and
> how your spiritual rights are being violated. I just
> wanted you to know I'll be plenty happy to fight
> on your side. I get all steamed up thinking of the
> wrong that's been done to you. If you'd like to
> hear more, put a lighted black candle in your bed-
> room window and I'll come a-running.

Arthur knew there was a lot to be said for not bringing any more gods into an already god-thickened situation. But he was stuck. No good alternatives had turned up
for him, even though he had wished and hoped for one
every night. So far, events did not favor the passive. That
could change any time, of course. The passive never gave
up the hope that the world was going to do something nice
for them. And the beginning of that something could be

this god with the scratchy name who was willing to fight for him.

Arthur thought, Yes, come and let's talk. Almost immediately there was a thickening of the air, and then a figure coalesced in front of him.

CHAPTER 39

ARTHUR'S CONVERSATION WITH SCABBER: SCABBER OFFERS his help. He'll destroy Leafie.

"Dexter sent me," Scabber said. "I'm here to help you."

"How can you do that?"

"Kill Leafie, the whole thing comes apart."

"Leafie looks pretty competent."

"Oh, I plan to kill him in an ambush."

"That's all right, then, I suppose. But he's not here in Florida, you know."

"He's not? Where's he gone?"

"To Portland," Arthur said. "That's Portland, Oregon."

Scabber gaped at him. It was getting complicated already.

"What's he doing there?"

"He went to watch the Blazers play in the NBA play-offs."

"What's that?"

"A popular sporting event."

"Is he staying somewhere around there?"

Arthur nodded. "I heard him mention he'd booked a room at the Marlowe Courts."

"That's good enough. Let me check my map."

Scabber took out his map and unfolded it to show North

America. He saw that Florida and Oregon were well separated and could be connected by a diagonal line, or by taking a more scenic route involving right and left turns.

"I'll just take care of this little matter," Scabber said, and disappeared.

Arthur wondered if he shouldn't have told Scabber that Leafie had brought a couple of other gods along with him. He supposed Scabber knew what he was doing.

Scabber flew high and fast over America, dipping down from time to time to check out landmarks. He spotted the Rockies without difficulty, took a right at the California coastline near San Diego, followed the coast up to Tillamook Bay, made another right turn, and there, revealed in a break in the clouds, was Portland.

The Rose Garden, the place where the sporting event was being held, was not difficult to find. Most of the humans in Portland were either inside the stadium or outside, buying and selling tickets.

Scabber landed in stealth mode. He asked a passer-by and learned he was close to the Marlowe Courts, where Leafie was staying.

He went there and asked the clerk if Leafie was in.

"Not today. He's gone to the victory celebration."

"What celebration's that?"

"How can you not know? The Blazers won the NBA championship last night, beating Chicago one-oh-two to seventy-eight. Man, did those guys fold up!"

"This victory celebration, where is it?"

"It's just past Multnomah Falls. It's being catered by the Rhinelander. Roast suckling pig, man!"

"How do I get there? Have you got a map? Thanks!"

En route, Scabber planned his strategy.

After the feast, Leafie could be expected to be in a stupor.

Scabber would attack him while he was sleeping. It looked like an ambush wouldn't be necessary. Killing a god while he was sleeping off a big meal was a well-proven tactic in the gods' book of treachery.

CHAPTER 40

LEAFIE HAD HAD HIMSELF SOME FUN AT THE BANQUET. FIRST there were his favorite Umpqua oysters, which he devoured by the bushel, shells and all, washing them down with entire barrels of choice microbrew. Next he put down a whole Columbia River salmon, twelve pounds, heads and guts included. After that, a barrel of microbrew, a roast suckling pig, a peck of fried potatoes, and then he had just enough room left for a few apple pies. Then he staggered off to sleep it off.

Scabber was able to use his short-range homing sense now. He came upon Leafie dozing after the feast, half submerged in the Columbia River, his arms resting on either shore.

Thinking to make a quick job it it, Scabber plucked a noble spruce from its bed in the forest and swung at Leafie's head with the rock-packed root.

It was a killing blow. Or would have been if there had not come a warning cry, high and tremulous, the warning cry of a god.

Damn it! Leafie had a god along with him.

It was Luuma, who had come along for the fun and was sitting in a nearby meadow devouring an entire Tillamook cow, hooves and all, thinking it an amusing way to get a drink of milk. She happened to glance up at the right moment and saw Scabber's monstrously swollen shadow across the sky. If the turnip-headed goddess hadn't instantly given a cry of alarm, Leafie's brains, such as they were, would have been scattered across the Cascades.

Hearing Luuma's cry, Leafie rolled out of the way, and the tree crashed down harmlessly, destroying the Bridge of the Gods and the cars still on it, but damaging the god not at all.

Leafie scrambled to his feet and beat a hasty retreat, Scabber following. Leafie went as far as the foothills of Mount Jefferson, where he plucked a boulder the size of a two-car garage and, with a single vast heave, threw it at Scabber. Scabber saw the thing coming through the air at him like a photomontage of an express train, dodged, and the boulder whistled by over his head and across the Columbia, smashing into the town of White Salmon and leveling several riverfront marinas.

Leafie countered by reaching up into an overhanging thunderhead and snatching the energy he found there, directing it to Scabber's arms, outstretched to grapple and wet from Oregon's constant rain. Lightning leaped and corruscated up and down Scabber's sides, burning him severely. Now Scabber was hard pressed.

His situation became worse when Luuma entered the fight, plucking the Timberline Lodge from the top of Mount Hood and throwing it at Scabber like a javelin. Scabber dodged, but a bronze weathervane pierced his right calf.

He wrenched out the projectile, but while he was doing so, Leafie gathered up a tangle of high tension wires and tangled Scabber in them.

Scabber tore himself free, but now Luuma was at him again, brandishing half a mile of railroad track she had torn up and was using as a flail. She cracked him a good one on the side of the head.

Scabber was stunned, fell back, tried to rally. But now

Rotte, god of treacherous warfare, appeared from out of nowhere, drawn by the scent of fighting, and flung himself on Scabber, burying his long fangs in Scabber's shoulder.

Scabber backed frantically away, Rotte hanging from him like an enormous limpet.

Scabber changed himself from a gigantic man-shape into a gigantic snake-shape, and rippled and shook his hide in an attempt to throw Rotte off. Leafie shouted encouragement and leaped onto Scabber's back, plunging his newly created talons into the god's hide on either side of the backbone.

Scabber screamed, a sound that shattered windows from Portland to Salem, and abruptly transformed himself into a small bat. Leafie and Rotte lost valuable moments looking around for him, before Luuma caught on and gave herself panoramic microscopic vision. Then she saw Scabber, winging away as fast as his leathery wings would take him.

Luuma changed into a buzzard and gave chase. Scabber winged back to Florida, the only place on Earth he knew, with Luuma and Leafie in hot pursuit, the three of them leaving vapor trails behind them of a size never before seen, and the sonic boom of their passage rolled diagonally across the United States.

Scabber evaded them, concealing himself in a thunder-head above Dade County. But then his strength was exhausted, and, wounded and bleeding, he fell to Earth, a glowing torch. His extra bulk, expanded for the fight, burned away as he fell. He lost his armor, his weapons, his amazing musculature. It was all consumed in that fiery descent. If the fall had been longer, perhaps he might have burned away entirely. As it was, the flaming atmosphere consumed him, his skin and meat, reducing him to a senseless skeleton as his brains bubbled out of his superheated skull. Even his bones glowed red hot, but they were not consumed, because gods' bones are not for the burning.

All during that long descent, the marrow in his bones had

been churning away, guided by his indestructible DNA, rebuilding nerves, brains, meat, skin, eyeballs, fingernails, the rate of new growth not quite keeping up with the burning, but close, close, until at last he fell to the ground with an ear-splitting crash, and while he lay there, unconscious, insensible, the process of rebuilding continued, until at last he was a humanoid figure again, but skinny, very skinny, stark mother naked and out of his mind with pain and anger and chagrin.

Consciousness returned and Scabber was able to see and hear, but he didn't know who he was or what had happened to him, for his brain's self-repair units, themselves newly recreated, were hard at work replacing and reconstructing his memory. And while this went on he was senseless and speechless, and knew only that he hurt and needed help.

It was night. He was lying on a suburban street. There were houses on either side. Street lamps cast pools of yellow light. The windows of some of the houses were lit. Scabber painfully dragged himself to the nearest house. It was brightly lighted. Scabber pulled himself onto the porch and staggered to a window. He tapped at it with his partially reconstructed fingertips, wincing at the pain.

A woman came to the window—a large, middle-aged woman wearing a flowered robe. She took one look at Scabber and stepped back, shrieking.

"Fred! Come quick! There's that Peeping Tom at the window!"

A brief delay. Sound of a chair scraping. Sound of a closet door behind opened. Rummaging sounds. The closet door slammed shut. A large middle-aged man came running into the living room. He wore blue jeans over which his paunch hung, and a Dolphins T-shirt. He was carrying a Louisville Slugger baseball bat.

"Where is the son of a bitch?"

"On the porch! Be careful, Fred!"

Fred threw open the front door and stepped out, bat

poised. Scabber, flat on his stomach, looked like something the cat had thrown up. He raised one imploring hand.

"Help . . . "

"Oh, I got help for you all right," Fred said, and brought the bat down with resounding force on Scabber's head. Scabber's head bounced twice on the porch, a two-beat heralding unconsciousness. Fred reared back for another shot.

"Fred, don't!"

"Why the hell not?"

"You know how these criminals are. He could sue you."

Fred arrested his swing. "Yeah, that's what they do, the bastards," he said. "Go call the cops. But if this one stirs a finger I'm going to fix him so he'll have to cop a plea in heaven."

The lady of the house went inside. Deep in Scabber's head, DNA churned in his newly reconstituted bone marrow, repairing his ruptured brain. By the time the police arrived, he was sufficiently in control of himself to disappear the hell away from there.

Scabber had never considered himself a deep thinker. He was in considerable distress at the moment, what with his brain still repairing itself and throwing up flash images of a dubious nature. Still, he realized that he was going to have to come up with something in order to accomplish his purpose. What could he come up with? He knew it would come to him in a moment, as soon as his headache passed.

CHAPTER 41

SCABBER LEFT EARTH AND RETURNED TO GODSREALM sore
and aching. His physical pains soon passed, since gods heal
quickly, and, as has already been noted, even reconstitute
themselves when destroyed. Scabber's defeat had therefore
caused him no long-lasting physical distress but his mental
anguish was considerable. He could still hear the howls and
laughter of Leafie and the others as they had chased him
across the Earth.

His agreement with Dexter could be considered void,
since he had tried and failed. But Scabber found something
within him which was unwilling to admit defeat, and which
was prepared now to dedicate itself to the task of revenge.

He checked among the minor gods, but found no takers of
his offer to lead them in a war against Leafie. Most gods are
lazy, and, when not actuated by strong emotions such as lust,
hunger, or envy, tend to lie around a lot and live aesthetically.
Not one single god or goddess was willing to throw in with him.

It seemed as though that would be the end of it. But Scabber was bold enough and motivated enough to take his peti-
tion to the High Gods.

They laughed at him, saying it was no business of theirs,
and that frankly it didn't matter a damn if he or Leafie got it

in the neck. There was little love lost between the High Gods and the low gods.

Scabber was stymied, but the desire for revenge burned brightly within him with a flame that would not die. And so he took an unprecedented step. He decided to consult a wise man. For when the gods are stymied, they often turn to humans for advice.

When a man has problems, he consults a god. When a god has troubles, he consults a man. This is the way it has always been. Each imputes to the other a wisdom he himself does not possess. And, so strange a place is the universe, each is frequently able to advise the other as to a likely way to proceed.

Where, however, was Scabber to find this wise man? Wise men's names are not published in a book, nor are they listed in the Yellow Pages. And in any event, Scabber dared not return to Earth without allies.

Scabber considered asking Dexter, the agent, who seemed to know a thing or two, but desisted, fearing that the agent was unhappy with him on account of his recent defeat.

Who else did Scabber know on Earth? Only Arthur. Scabber didn't know if Arthur was a wise man—there was no evidence for it one way or the other. But Arthur was the only man on Earth who had been able to contact a god for millenia. This argued in favor of his wisdom.

Scabber decided to try him out. Not in person, however. That was much too risky. Instead, he came to Arthur in a dream.

In this dream, Scabber took the form of a small furry animal, not quite a cat and not quite a dog, but something like both, a dogcat. He didn't have to be accurate about it; it was only a dream.

Gods of course are able to gain access to human dreams, though they rarely avail themselves of it, because if there's one thing a god finds boring it's talking to a human in a dream. In this case, however, Scabber had decided upon this consultation, and so he insinuated himself into Arthur's dream.

When Scabber came to call that night, Arthur was dreaming about Lapland, and Eskimos, and somehow a kangaroo had gotten mixed up in it, too. Arthur had been telling the kangaroo that he was really on the wrong continent and ought to get home when Scabber came waltzing in, disguised as a catdog, or dogcat, and said, "Since you're handing out advice, maybe you could advise me."

"Sure," Arthur said cheerfully, "what do you want to know?"

"I can't find my home," Scabber said in what he hoped would sound like a piteous tone. "Perhaps you could help me."

"Have you looked around?"

"I've looked all over Earth, and it's not here."

"Have you sought it in the heavens?"

"I have gone to the realm of the gods," Scabber said, "and what I seek is not there."

"You seem to have used up the available options," Arthur said.

"So it appears. Do you have any ideas?"

"Of course," Arthur said. "It's simple enough. If what you're looking for isn't among the humans or the gods of the humans, then it must be among the aliens."

"Aliens? What aliens?"

"I don't know," Arthur said. "You'll have to find that out for yourself."

"Aliens," Scabber mused. "Of course! What a good idea! You wouldn't happen to know where I'd find aliens, would you?"

"Not specifically," Arthur said. "But it shouldn't be too difficult. You must go to a place that is inhabited by intelligent living creatures who are neither gods nor humans. Odds are they'll turn out to be aliens."

"That's got to be it," Scabber said. "Thanks a million."

"Don't mention it," Arthur said, and returned to his dream of Lapland.

Arthur's dream then underwent several complications involving a coach run with harnessed mice, a beautiful lady who looked a lot like Mimi, a clarinet, and several other objects. By the time he awoke, all he remembered was the woman and the clarinet. Scabber disguised as a dogcat was long forgotten. Which was just the way Scabber wanted it to be.

CHAPTER 42

SCABBER WENT TO ONE OF THE UNEXPLORED REGIONS OF Godsrealm, where there were no known dieties. Scabber noted with approval the garish colors, the blasted heath, the strange amorphous shapes of everyday objects in this region, such as anthills and prairie dogs. Items like these were the unmistakable signs that he had come to a part of Godsrealm where an alien god lived. Even the sound of the wind in the upside-down trees was different.

And here he found the hermit god, a solitary diety who lived alone in this wild and abandoned place. This diety had put up a sign which read NO VISITORS WANTED. STAY OUT. THIS MEANS YOU. BEWARE THE MONSTER. DANGEROUS SPELLS LYING AROUND ARMED AND UNTENDED. THESE SPELLS ARE APT TO BLAST YOU. IF SO, THERE'S NO HELP FOR YOU. DON'T GO SNIVELING IF YOU GET CAUGHT IN ONE. YOU HAVE BEEN WARNED.

This was more than a little off-putting in one way, but more than a little encouraging in another, for it was proof positive that Scabber had reached an area of certified strangeness where he might hope to follow the advice of the prophet Arthur. So he continued, keeping a sharp outlook for monsters and spells. He passed a solitary raven, perched on a blasted tree trunk and croaking warnings of doom in a shivery voice. He walked past it, staying well away from its beak.

After a while he came to an area clearly marked ALIEN QUICKSAND OF THE MOST TREACHEROUS SORT — YOU HAVE BEEN WARNED!

He skirted it and came to clashing rocks, similar to the Symplegades, an alien construction occupying the very heart of classical mythology, a place where, for no imaginable reason, rocks advanced and crashed and thundered against one another. But it was easy enough to go around them.

Farther on, he came to a Scylla and Charybdis formation, another alien construction expropriated to classical use by generations of mythographers. Luckily, there was a suspension bridge over the formation. It was rickety, but Scabber negotiated it to safety.

After a while he came to a small mountain, and in the center of it was a cave. He was about to pass it by when he noticed, hanging from a tree in front of the cave, a bearskin. He approached. The bearskin had been cut and sewn into a sort of a cloak. Its presence argued that there must be someone around here.

He called out at the cave, "Is there anyone here?"

A voice from within called back, "No one here! Go away!"

"I know you're in there!" Scabber shouted.

There was a shuffling sound. After a few moments a small dwarf god came shuffling out of the cave. He was misshapen, ugly, and he had a scraggly beard that covered most of his face.

"Where'd you come from?" the dwarf god asked.

"From elsewhere in Godsrealm. I need to talk to you."

"Didn't you see my warning signs?"

"I noticed it, but I didn't think it necessarily pertained to me."

"How'd you get past the quicksand?"

"I walked around it."

"I knew I should have spread it around farther," the dwarf god muttered. "And obviously the clashing rocks didn't stop you, either."

"They were easy enough to get past."

"You should have seen them when I first put them up. Light and supple they were, and ever so fast. They would have mashed you into guacamole."

"That must have been quite some time ago," Scabber said.

"Yes, I guess it was," the dwarf god said. "No one ever comes this way, so I grew remiss."

"A bit of luck for me," Scabber said.

"I suppose you could think of it that way. Well, now you're here, what is it you want?"

"I want you to tell me about the aliens."

"I'm an alien."

"That's obvious. But you're an alien *god*. What I want to know about is alien *people*."

"What makes you think I'd know anything about alien people?"

"Just a hunch. That and the fact that you look weird and speak godspeak with an accent."

"It still shows after all these years," the dwarf god said. "Well, sonny, you're here now so I guess I'd better talk to you, all the sooner to get rid of you. Come on into my cave and we'll have a drink of bootleg soma that's better than anything you'll get back where you come from."

Scabber followed the dwarf god into the cave. The way in was narrow at first, but after a few dozen yards it widened out into a nice-sized room. There were several easy chairs, and the dwarf god motioned Scabber to sit in one.

"You got it furnished nice," Scabber said, looking around at the wall hangings, which were alien but pretty to look at.

"Just because I live alone don't mean I gotta live like a

pig." The dwarf god went to a stone shelf and took down a stone jug. He filled two stone cups and handed one to Scabber.

"Confusion to our enemies!" he said, and the two gods clicked cups and drank.

"It's good," Scabber said.

"Of course it's good. This here's home-brewed alien soma. You can't get this stuff in your stuffy gentrified realm of discourse."

They sipped for a few minutes in silent appreciation.

"Tell me about the alien people," Scabber said after a while.

"Nothing much to tell. They're a bunch of ingrates, just like humans. I gave them centuries of good service and what thanks did I get? They threw me out, that's what I got. Frankly, you can keep your alien people as far as I'm concerned."

"Humans are just as bad," Scabber said.

"I know it. Frankly, I don't give a curse for any living intelligent things at all, be they human or alien or something else."

"Is there something else?" Scabber asked.

"How should I know? I'm not the intellectual type. When my aliens threw me out, I came here. Godsrealm is a piss-poor place, but at least it's a place where a god can live undisturbed. Most of the time, that is."

"I apologize for disturbing you," Scabber said.

The dwarf god shrugged. "Apologies don't bunt a sceutem on the farashine."

"I beg your pardon?"

"It's an old alien saying. Untranslatable."

There was another few minutes' silence. Then Scabber asked, "What language do these alien people speak, anyhow?"

The dwarf god glared at him. "They speak proto-alien, of course. What else should they speak?"

"True, true. Could you tell me where I'd find these aliens?"

"On one of their alien planets, of course. Where else would they be?"

"Which planet?"

"It's easy enough to find alien planets," the dwarf god said. "They revolve around alien stars. Or is it rotate? I never can remember the difference."

"Which stars would that be?"

"Sonny, you must be unusually stupid. Alien stars are easy to find. They're the ones with alien names."

"Like for instance?"

"Betelgeuse. They don't come much aliener than that."

"Can you tell me another?"

"Algol."

"What about Canopus?"

The dwarf god glared at him. "Nothing alien about Canopus. Are you trying to pull my leg?"

"No, I really didn't know. Betelgeuse and Algol. I think that'll do for a start."

"What do you want to go talk to aliens for?" the dwarf god asked.

"I've got a few ideas I thought I'd try out on them," Scabber said evasively.

"Suit yourself. But don't forget the old saying: When you go to the alien gods, don't forget your striadus."

"What is a striadus?"

"I think I've answered enough questions," the dwarf god said. "This ain't no indoctrination course in alien peoples. If you've finished your drink, kindly do me the favor of getting the hell out of here."

"Just going," Scabber said, finishing his drink and putting down the cup on the stone coffee table. "Thank you for your help. I'm known as Scabber, by the way. I don't believe I got your name."

"They call me the dwarf god," the dwarf god said. "On your way out of here, don't step in the Trap of Tantalus."

"I'll watch out for it," Scabber said. "Good of you to mention it."

"I just don't want to hear your screams," the dwarf god said.

CHAPTER 43

SCABBER ASKED AROUND AND LEARNED THAT ALGOL IV
had at least one planet with aliens. Maybe more, but one
for sure.

He went there. The first thing Scabber noticed when he
arrived on Algol IV was the trees. They were low and bushy,
with gray-brown bark. They didn't look strange at all, and that
was good because Scabber hadn't known to what extent the
alienness of this planet extended. He was glad to see that the
trees looked like trees anywhere, and he patted one as he
went by it. The tree shivered and emitted a short burping
noise.

Scabber stopped, fixed the tree with a heavy glare, and
said, "What was that?"

"Excuse me," the tree said. "I just finished lunch."

Scabber let it pass. Maybe this place was a little more alien
than he first thought. So what? His business here wasn't with
the trees. He walked on, and found a narrow paved road that
led across a meadow and over a hill. He stepped on it and
began walking.

It was a fine day. Algol IV's sun, called Algol 0, and its tiny
dark companion Algol 0/1, were both visible in the dusky af-

ternoon sky. A slight breeze was blowing. There were purple dots in the air, caused most likely by the atmospheric diffraction, itself caused by the overloading of visual purple in the dark companion.

At ground level he found a squalid alien city with black light projectors mounted on tall W-shaped poles. In their glow, he was able to make out the luminous shapes of the inhabitants. He fell into conversation with one named Jabir.

"So tell me," the alien named Jabir said, "what are you doing here on our planet?"

"I guess it's a free galaxy," Scabber said. "I guess I can go where I please."

"I didn't mean it in a challenging way," Jabir said, for he knew Scabber was a god and therefore understood which side his salvation was buttered on.

"In what way did you mean it?" Scabber asked.

"I just wanted to know if there was something specific you came here for."

"Well, of course," Scabber said. "I'm a god. I always do things for a reason."

"That's what I figured. I knew right away you were a god."

"How'd you know that?"

"It's just something we aliens know when we're in the presence of a god. Now, what's your reason for coming here?"

"First let me ask you something," Scabber said. "Do you guys have by any chance an ancient myth about a god coming to you with promises of glory and revenge for unremembered wrongs?"

"Now that you mention it, yes, we do have such a myth."

"I thought so," Scabber said.

"Why do you ask?"

"Because I've got some news for you people. Take me to your populace."

"This could be something big," Jabir muttered. "Follow me." And he led the way toward the Great Plaza of the Revisitation of the Ancient One of Dreams, which was where newly arrived gods usually felt most comfortable.

PART 6

CHAPTER 44

SCABBER HAD MADE SOME INTERESTING DISCOVERIES ABOUT the aliens of Algol IV.

First of all, these aliens were bipedal quadropeds, the form nature has seen fit to use for all intelligent creatures. Well, not quite all. Some of these aliens were four-legged, two-armed creatures. These seemed to constitute the action arm of the alien forces. Other aliens had different forms entirely. Some were no more than big heads, looking like enormous misshapen pumpkins. These did not move at all. They grew in the ground, like plants, and they took nourishment from the soil. But they were also active animal-style eaters and needed cooked animal food for their intellectual development.

It was an interesting question how this adaptation had come about, since for many generations there was no one around to cook for them. Evolution had acted from future to past in this case, but it got its timing wrong, because many generations of pumpkin-headed aliens lived and died without the cooked animal foods they needed for their full high degree of intellectual development.

This did come about after a while, however, aided by the separately evolved two-legged forms of alien.

These two-legged aliens were much like humans in many

respects, except that their religion involved the worship of the pumpkin-headed ones.

The bipedal aliens went forth and searched all over their planet, looking for the pumpkin-headed ones. They didn't find them for a long time, however, because the pumpkin-headed ones were hidden in grottoes, and for many centuries the bipeds never searched in grottoes due to a built-in inhibition toward going into shady places.

Thus the evolution of the alien races was apparently brought to a standstill, until a prophet arose among them who conceived the idea of overruling the taboo and looking specifically in the grottoes. There they found what they had been looking for, the other alien ones whose existence had been separate but parallel with theirs for so long.

The first meeting between the two races had been recorded in sacred scriptures.

"Hello," the two legged-aliens said. "You are the great ones, are you not?"

"We have the happiness to be those creatures," the pumpkinheads said. "We have lived in quiet for a very long time, waiting for you to come along. Now that you've found us, it is only right that we enslave you utterly and that you spend your time serving us, for this is for the greater glorification of all aliens."

"Hear, him, hear him," the two-legged aliens said. "At last we have a racial purpose. What a small matter enslavement is when it can result in such joy."

And so came about the first rapprochement between the two main kinds of aliens, the heads and the limbs, as they called themselves.

The heads lost no time in setting out the diet they required for their proper intellectual development, and the limbs expressed their great joy at finally finding a higher good to be enslaved to.

A basis for social action was formed, and this made easier the detection of new forms of alien life as evolution saw fit to reveal them. These were sometimes found on mountaintops, sometimes in ocean bottoms, but they turned up in other places as well, such as inside certain large nuts, and in the upper canopies of deciduous trees.

Everyone was greatly pleased at the high degree of specialization these forms exhibited, for one of the nightmares of the aliens was the possibility of a general purpose creature such as man. Such a creature seemed to them a perversion of all that was right and decent in evolution, and so they were predisposed toward war with humans long before Scabber came to them and told about the humans.

Unfortunately, the humans were so stupid, to an alien's way of thinking, that they didn't know when they had been subverted, for humans were able to engage in contradictory behavior with the greatest of ease. Just when you thought you had a human or a nation of humans safely under your thumb (for aliens grew special thumbs in those days to have humans under) the silly creatures would forget all about their promises and go about killing you simply because you were different.

This was a gross irrationality, and the aliens hadn't known what to do about it until Scabber came along and suggested the idea of outright conquest. The aliens saw this as a natural idea whose time was long overdue. They got to work building space fleets and developing alien life-forms that would strike terror into the ranks of human beings. And this was convivial work for them, because they found they quite enjoyed striking terror.

CHAPTER 45

ON EARTH, MEANWHILE, AT THE PARTY AT ARTHUR'S PLACE, shortly after Asturas, Ahriman, and Cupid left, Mellicent felt something sharp prick her in the backside. She resisted the urge to scratch. She was a mannerly goddess, not like some of the sluts she could mention. She looked at Arthur, standing beside her. Strange how attractive this man suddenly looked to her. Even his slouch, which had repelled her at first, now seemed exuberantly boyish, engagingly louche. And his hang-dog expression, which she had just judged unfit for anyone to wear, god or mortal, now struck her as the epitome of beauty, the coquettish invitation of a male fawn already feeling his masculinity, throwing out his sly looks so that an impressionable female . . .

She stopped her train of thought with an effort. Damn it, she told herself, this isn't me thinking! Someone has gotten into my head and is thinking for me!

With that thought she took fright. She excused herself and went to the bathroom. Locking the door, she mobilized the self-protective autolocation unit in her mind that all gods and goddesses have, implanted before birth, a unit used to help a diety get back on the main track and not be swayed by the ephemeral currents of love or hate.

"Self-protection autolocation unit reporting."

"Something has caused a sudden change in my emotion-ality. Can you tell me if a foreign person has gotten control of my mind?"

"Negative," the unit said. "That's you yourself feeling those feelings."

"But how could that be? What has happened between one moment and the next?"

"You have been struck by Cupid's arrow, that's what," the unit said.

"Oh, no!" Mellicent cried. "Not that damned Cupid!"

"The very same."

"And not love!"

"Love, and you," the unit said. "Love and the weather, always together . . . "

She turned the unit off. This was no time for banali-ties.

Finding herself in love was the worst kind of bad news for Mellicent. Of all the stupid luck! She'd had plans, she was going to study dance under one of the graces, maybe sub as a muse. Now all that was over. She was in love with a *man*. A stupid human. It was worse than being pregnant. At least when you're pregnant you get a child out of it, but when you're in love, all you get is the foundering of your former hopes and plans.

She wasn't going to take it lying down. But first she had to get out of there in order to resist the temptation of seizing Arthur and smothering him with kisses, even though she de-spised him, so strange a thing is love.

Made to love against her will! And to love a man, of all things! There had to be something she could do about that.

Wounded dieties have an instinct to seek healing; and being wounded by love was no different from any other sort of grievousness.

Mellicent went to SABEAUT.

It had been decided a long time ago that the gods were too
impulse-ridden. It was all very well to talk of godlike whims
and caprices. But everyone knew a diety was known by his
steadiness, not his abberations into behavior not even a
human would want to call his own. Although high-class phi-
landerers like Zeus protested that their wayward amorousness
was part of their godlike character, in their own hearts, or in
their thumos, where the real action of thinking and feeling
took place, they knew the difference.

One of the most important distinctions between gods and
men is that men are isolated and forever thrown back on their
own resources, whereas gods have a backup system.

When a god finds himself in trouble of a psychological na-
ture, he knows just what to do: he calls the Supreme Advisory
Board for the Eradication of Adventitious and Unwanted
Traits. SABEAUT.

This is what Mellicent did as soon as she realized that
Cupid had harpooned her.

First she made her excuses, wanting to make a nice exit
from the party.

"Look," she said to Arthur, "it's been nice meeting you. I
gotta go now. See you around some other time, huh?"

"Sure," Arthur said.

Mellicent got out of there. She punched number six on
the keypad on her wrist, which was disguised as a bracelet. It
took her at once to Repair Row, as it was called.

Repair Row was a long, dingy street somewhere in Godsrealm.
No attempt had been made to beautify it. The gods and goddesses who came there had a lot more on their mind than ar-
chitecture and interior decoration. The place hadn't been
swept in a long time. Garbage lay in the gutters. The store-
fronts looked as though they had gone through a dust storm.

The overhead lighting flickered and cast a dull orange glow in which everyone looked ghastly. This was a place dedicated to seriousness, and it showed.

Mellicent went directly to the main offices of SABEAUT. The place didn't even have a storefront. Just a name and a sign pointing to a staircase.

Climbing the three flights, Mellicent came to a door. She pushed it open and entered a small reception room. Magazines lay in untidy messes on end tables that had seen better years. There was no one in the reception room except a receptionist, a large, severe lady with hair piled high on her head.

"How can we help you?" the receptionist said.

"I've been hit by Cupid's arrow," Mellicent said.

"How recently?"

"It must have been less than an hour ago. I came here as quickly as I could."

"Speed is of the essence in these matters," said the receptionist, pushing a button on her console. "Come inside." She led Mellicent into a room behind the reception room. There was a stretcher with wheels. She indicated to Mellicent that she should lie down on it. A door in another part of the room opened and in walked a tall young god with a short beard, dressed in a long white coat and with a reflector mounted on his forehead.

"Hit by a love arrow," the receptionist told him.

The doctor nodded, and even though his features remained impassive, Mellicent could tell by the lines that sprang up on his forehead that he considered it a serious matter.

He took an instrument from his pocket, set the gauge, and wound the flexible part around Mellicent's wrist.

"Are you checking my blood pressure?" Mellicent asked.

"No. This is a thumosifier. It checks the substrates in your ichor and removes them. I just hope we're in time."

"I came here as quickly as I could," Mellicent said.

The doctor shrugged. "You probably came as quickly as you *reasonably* could, which is a very different matter. You probably made your excuses to your friends or whoever was with you, paused to check your makeup, maybe even made a telephone call or two."

"No telephone calls," Mellicent said. "I came at once. But I didn't know I had to get here as fast as you're saying."

"If you'd seen as many cases of affection poisoning as I have, you'd have come here faster than fast." He unwound the flexible part of the thumosifier, read the gauge, frowned. "Yeah, you're poisoned, all right. But let's make absolutely certain. What's the first thing you think of right now?"

"Arthur Fenn," Mellicent said.

"That's the one to whom your love is directed?"

"Yes, it is."

"I don't know any god by that name."

"This is a mortal."

"Damn, that's really serious," the doctor said. "Loving a mortal is serious stuff for a goddess."

"Hey, don't I know it? Can't you do something for me?"

"It's too late to neutralize the poison by strabismic tituration. Your whole system is infected. We're going to have to try subrational displacement."

The doctor snapped his fingers. From hidden speakers came an old Earth song: "This Can't Be Love Because I Feel So Well." The subversive and insistent music hammered at her as the receptionist cranked the volume higher and higher. The back wall of the doctor's office faded and was replaced by a large sound stage with twinkling footlights. A team of dancers came out and began the Dance of Rationality. Their tightly controlled steps were accompanied by a light show of Cubist paintings. Mellicent felt herself swept into the dance. Almost without willing it, her feet took up the beat, her

hands moved gracefully above her head, and she twirled into
the dance.

The doctor stood at his console, punching buttons. A look
of utmost concentration covered his face like a caul. Quite absentmindedly he lighted a cigarette. It served to punctuate
what he was doing. The receptionist gave him an admiring
look, then, at a warning glance from him, resumed her blank
stare. It wouldn't do to show even the slightest expression of
that emotion they were trying to rid their patient of.

The music mounted to a climax. Mellicent twirled, dipped,
and moved in a trance of motion.

The receptionist whispered to the doctor, "I think it's
working."

"I think so, too," the doctor whispered back. "Now if we
can just get her out of here without reviving what we sought
to excise, we'll be doing real good."

"If anyone can do it, you can," the receptionist breathed.

"Get a hold of yourself," the doctor said.

Returning his attention to the console, he skillfully built
the music and effects to a tearing climax, and then went to a
sudden and ominous silence.

Mellicent stopped in midstep, looked around, and puz-
zled, asked, "What am I doing here?"

Concealing her glow of triumph, the receptionist gave
the standard response: "You came here to shop, my dear.
Aren't you through yet?"

The doctor, manipulating the keys of his console, had
changed the operating room into a boutique. There were
stands with dresses on them, cases with jewelry and precious
objects, racks of shoes, a separate section for swimwear.

Mellicent moved down the aisles, looking this way and
that, and wondering why the store personnel were all wearing
white coats and had reflectors on their foreheads. She looked
enquiringly at the receptionist.

"That's the latest look," the receptionist said, scowling at the doctor who hadn't gotten the setting quite right. "It's the Freudian look—kicky, isn't it?"

"I suppose so," Mellicent said absently. "Anyhow, there doesn't seem to be anything here I want."

She started toward the exit, and both doctor and nurse held their breaths. If she could just get out of this place without her memory being revived, she stood a good chance of being rid of her unwelcome love once and for all.

"Well, I'll be on my way," Mellicent said.

Just as he was about to go out the door, one case caught her attention. It was filled with jewelry. Nothing very fine, though the workmanship was more than adequate. Her gaze had picked out one item—a brooch, done in silver, with a delicate silver chain.

"This is quite nice," she said, taking the brooch and holding it up to the light.

"How the hell did that get there?" the doctor whispered to the receptionist.

"How the hell should I know?" the receptionist whispered back snappishly.

And there was another snap, this one quite subdued, as Mellicent opened the brooch.

Within was the photograph of a man with an undershot jaw, small lidded eyes, and an ineradicable air of vagueness.

"Oh, Arthur!" she said. "How could I have forgotten!"

"Bad luck," the doctor said. "Mellicent, I'm afraid there's nothing more we can do for you."

"I suppose not," Mellicent said in a hopeless voice. "Anyhow, thanks for trying."

She exited.

The doctor turned to the receptionist. "I want to know who put that brooch there. And who put the photograph in the brooch."

"I'll get right on it," the receptionist said. But an answer was never found. And if it had been, it would have done Mellicent no good. Even the gods are subject to unexplained anomalies.

CHAPTER 46

HAPPY INDEED WAS SCABBER WHEN, LOOKING AROUND HIM, he saw the massed ranks of aliens who had come together to greet him. They had gathered in their tens and hundreds of thousands, swelling rapidly to their millions, in the great space known as Forbidden Square.

This square, in the heart of the main city, was some twelve miles to a side, and was equipped with loudspeakers mounted on tall standards and shrouded in a nearly indestructible transparent white plastic pierced to allow for ventilation. An alien called Xose explained that these covers protected the loudspeakers from the elements during the long years and longer centuries in which they had stood unused.

"Unused?" Scabber asked. "You mean, used never?"

"That is precisely what I mean," Xose said.

"I do not understand," Scabber said.

"It is simple enough. The great Forbidden Square is one of the oldest artifacts of our civilization, dating back to a time no alien can remember, always held in sacred trust, and never used, kept strictly out of bounds, with dire penalties for whoever would be rash enough to disregard the warning and step into its sacred precinct."

"Didn't you even test the loudspeakers?"

"We did not. But our ancestors wrought well, and we had no doubt that they would work when the great day came and they were to be used."

"Are you telling me," Scabber said, "that your remote ancestors built this square and its loudspeakers not to use themselves, but to await the arrival of a certain day in the future?"

"That is precisely what I mean," Xose said. "For a god who has spent so much time among humans, you show a keen understanding of our ways."

"Thank you," Scabber said, "but how did your ancestors know what they were building for?"

"They didn't," Xose said. "But they were born with the knowledge of how to build this square, knowledge already in their genes, put there, we doubt not, by some remote future descendent who desired to have things come out a certain way upon a certain occasion."

"And how do you know this is the occasion?"

"Our very DNA sings to us," Xose said. "With your arrival, our destiny has been made manifest. We are to go off to war against the humans, and are to lead us."

"Well, yes, that's what I came here for," Scabber said. "But it surprises me that you would have been awaiting my arrival."

"Our people in the future are sure to be much cleverer than they are nowadays," Xose replied. "You shouldn't wonder that they foresaw this glorious eventuality and made arrangements so that it should come to pass."

"But if your descendants in the future knew that this was to take place," Scabber said, "then it must have taken place already for them to know it. Is that not so?"

"That would seem to be the case," Xose said, "unless you took into account the dream development of a race as opposed to its realtime development."

"Ah, I see," Scabber said, though he didn't.

"And now, if you please, the people await your words."

Scabber stepped up to the microphone and tested it with

a thumbnail. It gave forth a satisfying amplified thump. The aliens cheered, and you could hear some of them saying, "It is the veritable mark of the god—the Testing of the Microphone!"

And another replied, "That I should live to see this day!"

And a third said, "If you don't stop stepping on my foot you'll not live to see another."

But this and other good-natured badinage fell to silence as Scabber stepped forward and cleared his throat.

"Friends and fellow aliens," Scabber said, his voice booming boisterously across the great square and rebounding off the amplifying boards set into its periphery, boards made of rarest lignum sonae and so designed as to give even those farthest from the loudspeakers a full measure of his godlike voice, "I consider myself every bit as much an alien as you when it comes to essentials, which I'll not go into at this time but which we may take up at our leisure. I am most happy to stand here before you, your very own god, elected by that prescient element in your germ plasm which anticipated my arrival and made preparations for it . . . "

Scabber hesitated, laughed, and said, "I seem to have lost the beginning of my sentence!"

"How like an alien!" the aliens said in a good-humored way.

"Ah yes, I remember now. I was about to tell you what plans I have for you. My very dear friends, those plans planted in my germ plasm as well as yours. My plans call for the immediate and expeditious destruction of that planet which calls itself Earth, and which is inhabited by those creatures who call themselves human beings!"

"Damned cheeky of them," a voice in the crowd said in commentary. "Say on, oh most excellent god, for we'll listen with baited breath and perked ears, and those of us who are hearing-disadvantaged will be instructed by the hearing-enabled among us, who have come equipped with slate gray chalkboards and white lustrous chalk for this very purpose."

"That is a response most laudable," Scabber said. "But let us not waste time in further palaver. So now you will proceed from this spot, in an orderly manner, to the place where the spacefleet is located, and there embark forthwith and with no delay, for there is not a second to be lost in the perpetration of so august an enterprise."

"Hear him! Hear him!" the aliens shouted, and so, in orderly ranks, they proceeded, with Scabber at their head, through the city and down to the dim desolate fields where a spacefleet had been laid down from remotest times by their prescient ancestors, and kept safe in transparent ventilated white plastic dropcloths until such time as they would be needed.

Scabber was pleased to note that the ships, though ancient in terms of years, yet had about them that air of modernity which can only be brought forth by ancestors dreaming the future. He was surprised by the great variety of shapes that met his eye. They were too numerous to enumerate, yet begged an explanation all the same.

"I see you are surprised at the differently shaped spaceships we have," Xose said. "Our ancestors laid it down that there should be a shape of ship to fit each shape of alien. And so it has come about."

"Your ancestors were most prescient in their appreciation of what the future would require," Scabber said. "Are the pilots, the navigators, the cooks and clean-up persons, the soldiers, the marines, the women's support corps, and, in fine, everything required for an expedition of this size and moment here assembled?"

"They're here and ready," Xose said.

"Then let's get on with it," Scabber said. "Aliens! To your ships! Chief astrogator! Report to me and I'll give you a course that will lead to the ineluctable moment of destiny."

Xose stood proudly to attention. "I am your chief astrogator. Your ship, my lord, awaits you. Note that it can only be described as godly."

Scabber did indeed note it. It was a great golden ship, and, with the white plastic coverings stripped from it, it shone forth with an effulgence which vied with that of the small dim dwarf sun that had lighted the whole enterprise.

"We will take the lead," Scabber said to his astrogator. "Let the others follow in whatever order pleases them best."

"It shall be so accomplished," the astrogator said. And soon, very soon, and with surprising celerity, the entire space-fleet took to the skies, where they circled once around the home planet, and then, as Scabber instructed, plunged into the secrecy and shrouded mystery of subspace, with the intention of emerging within striking distance of the planet Earth.

CHAPTER 47

"Hi," Mellicent said. "I'm back."

Arthur had been sitting in his bedroom drinking his morning coffee when Mellicent arrived behind his back. He jumped involuntarily, spilling coffee over the front of his dressing gown.

"Damn!" he said. "Sorry. You startled me, Mellicent, coming at me that way. Isn't there some way you could announce your arrivals? Ring a bell or something?"

"Listen," she said. "I have something important to say to you."

Arthur had that feeling of unfairness a man gets when he's about to be reproached by a goddess he barely knows.

"Whatever it is," Arthur said, "I'm sorry."

"For heaven's sake, shut up and listen to what I have to tell you."

"Oh, sorry," Arthur said again. "What is it, Mellicent?"

"Arthur, I love you."

"Oh . . . that's nice."

"And I have decided that we will live together and I will let you worship me."

"Oh . . . gee, that's great, Mellicent."

"You don't seem pleased."

"Of course I'm pleased. How could I not be pleased?"

"I don't know, but you're not. Arthur . . . could it be that you don't love me?"

"Hey, of course I love you," Arthur said indignantly. "Whoever said I didn't?"

Mellicent was about to do she didn't know what when a thought suddenly occurred to her.

"Oh," she said.

"What is it?" Arthur said.

"I just realized that just because I love you doesn't mean you love me."

"Of course it does!" Arthur said.

"Just a minute," she said.

"Yes?" Arthur said, cringing.

"Don't be afraid, I won't hit you. Stop cowering."

"Yes, ma'am."

"And don't call me ma'am."

"No . . . Mellicent."

She sighed. "You don't love me. Not one little bit. What a fool I've been! I've been assuming that just because I loved you . . . but you don't love me, do you? The truth now, Arthur!"

"I respect you tremendously," Arthur said. "I think you're the most beautiful thing I've ever seen."

"But you don't love me."

"No, I guess not."

"Good-bye, Arthur."

CHAPTER 48

MELLICENT WENT BACK TO GODSREALM, LOOKING FOR ADVICE from one of the senior goddesses, Aphrodite, who lived in a drafty Parian marble temple near the Vale of Tempe region.

Aphrodite gave her tea and offered sympathy.

Aphrodite said, "No one likes being made to fall in love. Love is a typically male idea. Only a man could have thought of it. Only a masculine principle in the universe could have contrived it so that it could happen at all."

"I never knew you felt that way," Mellicent said.

"Do you think I've enjoyed being chief goddess of love? Not a bit of it! It's just been a long series of infatuations with one conceited bum after another. And they all left me after a while. When he's finished with love, a man or a god looks for something else to do."

"I don't think Arthur would be that way."

"Love is misery whether a man does as he's told or not. It's misery when he leaves you and its misery when he hangs around and outwears his welcome."

"Since you know all that, I'm surprised you didn't find some way to use it to your advantage."

Aphrodite shrugged. "What is a goddess of love who has been programmed by the masculine principle of the universe to do? Love is her only enjoyment. Although it may be intellectually dishonest, without it there's no pleasure, no reason to live."

"I know," Mellicent said. "I want to go to the guy so bad it hurts. But I also want to be free of him. What do you advise?"

"Forget about getting free of love. You're stuck, kid. Cupid's shots are final, they can't be repealed. You might as well relax and enjoy it."

Mellicent made a face. "But who could enjoy the love of a mortal?"

"Hey, there are some pretty nice mortals," Aphrodite said. "I remember that boy Paris."

"Arthur is no Paris."

"Whatever. The principle's the same."

"Well," Mellicent said, "if I gotta live with it, I guess I gotta. It's beneath my dignity to let a mortal embrace me, but I'll make an exception this time. But I'll make sure Arthur knows the once-in-a-lifetime deal he's getting when he gets me."

She hurried off. Aphrodite drank tepid tea and marveled to herself at how much this young Mellicent had to learn. If Mellicent thought being in love was tough, wait until she got a look at being loved; or, as was likely in this case, not being loved.

CHAPTER 49

MELLICENT RETURNED TO THE VALE OF TEMPE IN GODSREALM. Her father was in the garden, tending the vines. She told him about how this mortal has spurned her.

Simus straightened up and said, "How could he have? Wasn't he hit by a love arrow?"

"No, I told you. He wasn't. I was."

"Then how can you expect him to be in love with you?"

Mellicent was indignant. "He ought to love me because I'm beautiful and a goddess."

"My poor girl, haven't you learned yet that not even gods love for good reasons, and even less so men? Anyhow, why should he love you? Is it an enjoyable thing, this love?"

"Definitely not," Mellicent said.

"Then why should he enjoy loving you? Why should he love you at all, unless he's forced to, just like you were?"

She stared at him. "Oh. I think I'm starting to understand what you mean. But isn't there any way to get Cupid to strike him, too?"

Simus shook his head. "Not a chance. Cupid hates reciprocity. He likes things one-sided."

"Well, what can I do?"

"Try to get along, my girl. It's the only thing left us in the end."

"But why should the end have come so early for me?"

Father had no comment on that.

CHAPTER 50

MELLICENT FOUND HERMES PUTTING A COAT OF WAX ON HIS lyre.

"I need some advice," Mellicent said.

"Shoot."

"I'm in love with this mortal and he doesn't love me."

"Sounds normal enough to me," Hermes said. "What's the difficulty?"

"I want him to love me."

"Have you tried all the wiles of seduction?"

"Yes, I have."

"What about the wiles of nonseduction?"

"What do you mean?"

"Pretending the opposite of what you feel."

"You mean, lying?"

"Precisely."

"I'm above that."

"Too bad. Then you'll never get what you want."

"There must be a way!"

"There is. I've just told you about it. It is called dissimulation. It means pretending other than what you feel."

"What a loathsome idea!"

"You're right," Hermes said. "Don't do it. Better to be true to oneself than to be loved."

"No, that's not what I want."

"Well, lady, if you want what you want, I've told you how to go about getting it. If you don't want it that much, go away and do something else."

And with that Mellicent had to be content.

Mellicent returned to Earth. She moved back into Arthur's bedroom without saying a word about her absence.

Arthur told her again how sorry he was that he didn't love her.

"That's all right, I don't really give a damn about that. I just want to hang around to watch the action."

"The action?"

"Sure. This is the liveliest spot in two worlds."

Arthur was disturbed, though he knew he really shouldn't care. He was just beginning to notice that Mellicent was very attractive. He thought it strange he hadn't noticed it before.

Mellicent hadn't really stopped loving Arthur, of course. She loved him even more madly than before. But with the imperative to love had come the knowledge of how to make love work. Or how to work love. Lying and dissimulation were definitely some of love's better weapons.

Some say she learned this on her own. Others say she was instructed by Hermes.

She knew it was pretty small potatoes, letting herself be loved by something as insignificant as a human being. But it was better than nothing at all.

CHAPTER 51

ON PAPER AT LEAST, MELLICENT WAS THE MOST WONDERFUL
thing that had ever happened to Arthur. But that wasn't saying much, since Mellicent would have been the most wonderful thing that could have happened to any man. A goddess
is to a woman as Hyperion to a satyr; and a love goddess is to
an ordinary goddess as . . . well, she simply beggared all com-
parisons, and no figure of speech was contrasty enough to
catch one-tenth of the full flavor of Mellicent, beautiful young
love goddess of the ancient Syrians, modern love goddess of
Arthur Fenn.

However, it has also been noted that it takes a man of considerable powers, monumental sensuality, and a sense of dis-
crimination finer than that of a professional wine taster to
really appreciate a goddess. Unfortunately, Arthur Fenn was
none of those things. Sensuality and discriminationwise, he
was a pretty ordinary dogsbody of a man. Mellicent was wasted
on him.

She knew it, too, but was thoughtful enough never to
mention it, except by inference now and again when she was
fed up. And Arthur gave her much to be fed up about.

When she came closer than a foot or so to him, Arthur
started trembling. He fainted at her touch.

This was highly flattering in a way, but did not conduce toward that grand sexual consumation that Mellicent was created for. Consumation was in fact completely out of it. Arthur was too filled with awe, respect, self-hatred, and low self-esteem to touch her, or allow her to touch him.

Not that she was about to make the first advances. Goddesses, though they have nothing against aggression, prefer to be wooed in the normal fashion, with men making the overt moves. In Arthur's mind, however, any thought of a physical approach was tantamount to lèse-majesté, and not far short of blasphemy.

No matter how often she told him, he just couldn't get it through his head that she desired him. He always asked himself, who am I to be desired by a goddess? and the answer always came back, a poor schnook, that's who you are. Such thoughts don't lead to successful wooing.

Mellicent saw his difficulty. She was wise in the ways of men, having boned up on it in a hurry, and she knew low self-esteem when she saw it. She decided to bide her time, give Arthur a chance to get used to her.

She thought about Hermes's advice and decided to seek further council. She arranged a talk with Minoche, who had once been a high god of the Lebanese. She and Minoche had been friendly for a long time, and she respected the older god's wisdom.

"I've got a problem," she said to him one day, after seeking him out in his ranch in west Godsrealm.

"I should think so. There's a faint frown on your perfect brow. You must not let difficulties mar your looks, my dear."

"Then help me out of my difficulties."

She told Minoche how she had fallen in love with a mortal man, and had gone to him, and how this man had shunned her, and seemed to be in awe and fear of her.

Minoche said, "Have you ever loved a mortal before?"

"No, I have not," Mellicent said. "The thought never occurred to me."

"To each his own is a good rule," Minoche said. "But what you're experiencing has happened from time to time, and there have always been difficulties. These difficulties have always been on the part of the human."

"He seems to feel inferior to me," Melicent said.

"And well he should. He is a mere human person. You are a goddess."

Mellicent sighed. "What can be done about that?"

"Oh, there's a way. I'm surprised you haven't thought of it yourself."

"Tell me!"

"You must listen carefully, my dear. In what I am going to say there are certain risks, but the results can almost be guaranteed. Have you thought of giving him a present?"

"*He* should be showering *me* with presents!"

"Of course, my dear. But I had in mind a present for him of a most special and unusual kind. The sort of gift that only a goddess can bestow . . . "

"Arthur," Mellicent said that evening, when they were alone.

"Yes, my love?" Arthur said.

"I have a present for you."

"That's terribly good of you," Arthur said. "But you really shouldn't have."

"Aren't you going to ask me what it is?"

"I'm sure you'll tell me in your own good time."

Mellicent sighed. This deferential quality Arthur had could really be annoying at times. But she was determined to be nice.

"Here it is, my dear." She took a small box from her bosom and presented it to Arthur.

Arthur turned it over and over in his hands, mumbling, "It's beautiful, simply beautiful . . . "

"Open it up."

"Oh. I was going to do that, of course."

He opened the box. Inside there was a ring. It appeared to be made of iron and was quite simple, though with curious runes engraved on it.

"Oh, it's just beautiful," Arthur said, in so fatuous a tone that Mellicent could have kicked him.

"Put it on."

"Well, I'm not sure I ought to. Is it safe?"

"Arthur," Mellicent said, in a tone in which she could not entirely keep out a note of menace, "it is not safe for you not to."

"Oh, very well," Arthur said. He slipped the ring on his index finger, where it fit nicely. "And now?"

"Now I think you'd better lie down for a while," Mellicent said.

"But why should I do that?"

"The ring has certain . . . properties. They take getting used to."

Arthur suddenly turned pale. "I felt something!" he said.

"Yes," Mellicent said, "I should think so."

"Something in my stomach."

"That's where the first effect is often experienced."

"The first effect of what? Mellicent, what did you put in that ring?"

"Nothing bad, my dear. Go lie down for a while. You'll be pleased, I promise you."

Arthur went and lay down. Mellicent went to her own corner of the room and picked up a fashion magazine. Twenty minutes later she was studying the latest Paris creations when Arthur rose from his bed.

"Yes?" she said, not looking up.

"Mellicent, what have you done to me?"

"What makes you think I've done something to you?"

"Look at me!"

Mellicent put down the magazine and looked him over. He had had to change his clothes, because now he was a bigger man by far. He stood well over six feet, and was proportionately broad. His hair, formerly a dull mouse brown, was now golden and wavy. Even his features had been reshaped. To put it in a nutshell, he looked like a nerd when he put on the ring and now he looked like a superstud.

"Do you like it?" Mellicent asked. "It's my little gift to you."

"But what did you do?"

"I gave you the appearance and powers of a demigod," Mellicent said.

"Me? A demigod?"

"Look at yourself."

"Appearance is one thing. But a real demigod has powers unavailable to ordinary humans."

"Check it out," Mellicent said. "You will find that you are preeminent in weapons as well as unarmed combat; that you have an encyclopedic knowledge of the more useful spells; and a lot more besides."

"A lot more? What lot more?"

"Your capacity has been expanded in all areas," Mellicent said demurely. "If you get what I mean."

"Do you mean what I think you mean?"

She quickly read his mind, something she normally avoided because it was intrusive and not good manners. But it seemed all right just this once.

"Yes," she said, "you are right in thinking that you now have unexcelled capacity for the most delightful things in life, as well as an enhanced ability to enjoy them."

"Wow!" Arthur said.

"Yes, isn't it?" Mellicent responded.

A moment later he was bending over her and lifting her up in his brawny arms.

"Woman," he said, and his voice was half an octave deeper than it had ever been even when he had a cold, "this is the moment we have been waiting for."

"Yes," Mellicent said. "Oh, yes!"

They fell into each other's arms.

But not long after that, they were both sitting on Arthur's bed, naked, two splendid naked animals with nothing passing between them but frustration.

"Damn!" Arthur said.

"What went wrong?" Mellicent asked.

"I don't know. When it came to the actual moment . . . I was simply unable."

CHAPTER 52

AND SO LIFE WENT ON. RELATIONS BETWEEN ARTHUR AND Mellicent were strained. Leafie and the others congratulated Arthur on his new enhanced appearance, and told him he was a lucky dog to have a goddess as beautiful as Mellicent at his beck and call.

Arthur didn't contradict them. He didn't discuss Mellicent and his problems with her with anyone. Let them think what they wanted to think.

Everyone seemed to think he was a lucky dog; except for Mimi, who, coming in to work one day in her new role as high priestess of NARWAG, looked him up and down, sniffed briefly, and asked him if he weren't putting on weight, and if he had begun to use perfume. Arthur didn't use perfume, of course, nor even aftershave lotion. As for putting on weight, he knew very well he was solid muscle. Mimi's remarks had been intended to woo him, which another man might have considered her way of still showing interest in him, but which Arthur interpreted as a further sign of her undying dislike of him. He ignored her and went about his business.

There was a lot to do those days. The cult had grown with amazing rapidity, and now had chapters in forty states, with new ones signing on every day, and with an international following as well. Arthur's was supposed to be the last word on doctrine and ritual. He paid very little attention to his duties, however, and usually signed whatever papers were put forth in his name without bothering to read them. He was aware, in his own dim fashion, that Leafie's god friends were playing hell with the Earth.

Arragonet, a newly arrived nature god, had conceived it his duty to arm the Earth and its growing things against the depredations of mankind. He had come up with a grass that could grow anywhere and was almost impossible to kill. It choked out everything else.

Not even the gods approved of this. They remonstrated with Arragonet, who replied, "A god's gotta do what a god's gotta do."

Leafie finally had to bring in Yrtys, the proto-Babylonian god of fire, to cut back this growth of supergrass that was choking off the more useful plants. Yrtys was successful in devastating whole hundred-mile-square blocks with his fire, burning it so completely that the grass could never grow again. But nothing else could grow again, either.

There were a lot of other bad effects from the actions of the gods. They simply couldn't resist tinkering with the balance of things on Earth, and their pompous blundering brought even worse results on mankind. Leafie and some of the other, more socially minded gods tried to offset this by miraculous dispensations, feeding entire populations with a food they called manna brie. But they soon got tired of this, and besides, it would take a god working full time just to supply burgeoning mankind with what it needed.

None of the gods had time for this; they had more important fish to fry. So the situation for Earth continued, no better; in fact, getting a lot worse.

CHAPTER 53

ONE DAY MILLICENT SAID TO ARTHUR, "I'VE BEEN MEANING to speak to you about something that has me a little upset."

"Let's talk, by all means," Arthur said, his heart sinking.

"You have claimed since my return that I am your ideal woman."

"That's what I've said and what I mean," Arthur said. "You are the most beautiful, the most desirable woman or goddess I or any man could conceive. I only regret the incapacity that does not permit me to enjoy what would be with you the greatest of pleasures imaginable."

"So you say," Mellicent said.

"And so I mean."

"In that case, could you explain to me why you dream of other women?"

"I do no such thing," Arthur said, lying instinctively and magnificently.

"I am very much afraid I must tell you that is a lie."

"It is not!" Arthur retorted hotly. "I guess I know better than anyone what it is I dream."

Mellicent stared at him for a moment, then said, "Oh, Arthur, you are so transparent!"

"Why do you say so?"

"Because I have been monitoring your dreams, and they are about quite a few women, but nowhere in them do I find me."

"You've been monitoring my dreams?"

"Yes. That is one of the abilities of a goddess."

"I think it is very unfair of you."

"Well you might say so when you use your dreams to escape from me and go to the imagined charms of other women."

"You must have gotten it wrong," Arthur said, lying valiantly. "I dream only of you, when I dream at all."

"Is that so? Then how do you explain these?"

Mellicent took a packet of glossy prints out of her purse and handed them to Arthur.

"What are these?" Arthur asked.

"We gods have our own ways of learning about the dreams of mankind, and we had this ability long before your invention of the camera. These are metaphysical snapshots of your dreams over the last two weeks. Look at them and deny that they are true."

Unwillingly, Arthur looked. The pictures portrayed him in a variety of lewd poses with a great variety of women, among whom most prominently was Mimi.

"I have no control over my dreaming!" he said angrily. "And it is unfair and unkind of you to invade my privacy in this way."

Mellicent shrugged. She, like the other gods, cared not a fig for fairness. "You are unfaithful to me in your very heart of hearts!" Mellicent said. "Good-bye, Arthur." And with an imperious gesture, she disappeared.

PART 7

CHAPTER 54

MEANWHILE, IN THEIR OWN ETHEREAL REALM, THE HIGH
Gods lay around in a state of torpor. One of them, Lasca, had
been asked to watch for late-breaking developments. He kept
watch on a high crag, from which he could get a panoramic
view of Earth and its vicinity.

He saw something down there in space that made no
sense to him. It was lights, a lot of little lights, and they were
moving over the black velvet of space toward Earth.

As he sat on the hillside, an oracular blackbird came to
him, its wings bedraggled, breathing hard.

"I've got news," the bird said.

"Tell," Lasca replied.

"You been watching what's going on down there?"

"What is it?"

"An alien spacefleet of enormous size is approaching
Earth."

"Aliens? You did say aliens?"

"That's what I said."

"Aliens aren't supposed to enter into things," Lasca said.
"Not at this time, at least. Are you sure you got it right?"

"Of course. I'm no dodo."

"Aliens attacking Earth is very bad news indeed," Lasca said. "How did this come about?"

"Well, it's a long story," the bird said. "There's this god Scabber. He's leading them."

"I know about Scabber. He was brought into the game by Dexter, who in turn was working for our fellow High God Asturas."

"True enough. But you haven't taken into account Ahriman."

"Ahriman? Who's that?"

"Asturas's evil younger brother."

"Oh. Go on."

"This Asturas didn't want to save the universe. He looked for ways to help bring about it's dissolution. He joggled Cupid's elbow, causing him to shoot a love arrow into Mellicent."

"Mellicent? I know I've heard that name before."

"Syrian love goddess."

"Right, go on."

"Well, then, this Ahriman, looking for another way to cause trouble, saw Dexter looking for someone in Godsrealm to help Arthur."

"Arthur?"

"The human who started all this trouble."

"Right, okay."

"So Ahriman went to Dexter, who was trying to help Arthur, and, pretending to be a friend, advised him to choose Scabber as Arthur's champion. Dexter thought the god was doing him a good turn. So he contacted Scabber and brought him in on Arthur's side."

"Scabber!" Lasca said. "Of all the gods to choose!"

"Sure," the bird said. "You know that and I know that. But Dexter didn't know that. He didn't know he was being given a bum steer."

"I know what happened after that. Scabber got defeated

by Leafie, as was perfectly predictable, and went out for his revenge. He got to the aliens somehow—"

"Arthur advised him to seek them out."

"Oh, no!"

"He didn't know what he was saying, of course. But now we've got Scabber leading a huge horde of aliens in spaceships against Leafie and his friends."

"The aliens versus the gods," Lasca mused. "It would be a fit theme for an ironic poem."

"There's no time for poetry," the bird told him. "You can figure out for yourself what's going to happen next."

Lasca had no difficulty making the prediction. This encounter of titanic forces was likely to destroy the Earth and its inhabitants. And that had not been the universe's intention.

"I'll go and tell the others," Lasca said.

The High Gods listened to what Lasca had to say and agreed that the situation was serious. They called up Asturas to see if there wasn't something he could do about his brother.

"I didn't know until too late that my own brother was acting the traitor in regard to the course of events I was born to serve. How's that for a subject for a five-act tragedy?"

"Forget the tragedy," Lasca said. "Can you do something about it?"

"You bet I can," Asturas said, and raced off to find his brother.

When Asturas found his brother, Ahriman was sprawled across a galactic cloud, watching the alien spacefleet speeding toward Earth.

"Pretty sight, don't you think?" he said.

"Turn them back," Asturas said.

"And how do you suppose I could do that?"

"Put a suggestion into the mind of your creature, Scabber, the one who's leading this mess. Make him abort this operation."

"And why should I do that?"

"Because Earth will be destroyed if you do not."

"That's fine by me," Ahriman said.

"And if Earth goes, so goes the universe."

"Stands to reason," Ahriman said.

"We must do something!"

"Not me. I serve the other side. I'm going to tear this universe down around your ears, brother. Then we'll see who's firstborn the next time we come around."

"I won't have it!" Asturas said, and leaped for his brother.

Ahriman had been waiting for that. His response was instantaneous.

The two brothers grappled and struggled. So closely were they matched that neither could gain an advantage. And their reserves of energy were so abundant that there was no reason for the fight to end any time in the foreseeable future.

Their struggle went on interminably.

The alien fleet continued to move toward Earth.

CHAPTER 55

It was early morning — a peaceful time for gods and men. Arthur was sitting in a corner of his bedroom with *The New York Times* crossword puzzle. Life had improved for him since he'd been able to get the *Times* airmailed to his home each morning. Many luxuries are possible for one who is a prophet of the world's fastest-growing religion. Arthur was not much for luxuries, but he did like his morning *Times*.

A dim light flashed in a corner of his room. By itself, the light was nothing much to speak of. Yet even a person more obtuse than Arthur might have recognized the peculiar signature of that light which marked it as coming from no earthly source. Arthur so marked it, but it didn't alarm him or even warn him of things to come, for he had become accustomed to strange manifestations during his intense association with the minor gods.

There was a sound as of trumpets, high and piercingly sweet. This might have warned him. But it did not.

Arthur had become blasé to strange manifestations. When you consort with the gods, out-of-body experiences are like your daily bread and butter. Therefore he took no heed of either light or sound, but instead applied himself to his crossword puzzle. But therein was the first symptom of the matter that was coming into being which would wise him up to a new situation entirely.

As he scanned his crossword for matters he could fill in without undue cerebration, he noted that 59 across, eight letters, beginning with "G," read: "The characteristic sign that a godlike or enhanced being wants a conference with you." He stared at it, not remembering that it had not been there before. And the definition came into his head: Godcall!

It began to dawn on him that a preternatural situation was shaping up, and that it was directed at him. He put down his pencil, rose to his feet, and from beside his bed he picked up the small backpack that he had prepared over a week ago, when he had had a presentiment of such things as this taking place.

Then, with a great whoosh of wind and a glaring of light, Dexter appeared in front of him.

"It's all over," Dexter said.

"What do you mean? What's all over?"

"Everything!"

"Can't you be more specific?"

"I picked the wrong god. Ahriman convinced me to try him. I did. And now the fight between Scabber and his aliens and Leafie and his allies is inevitable. This battle will destroy Earth. The universe is going to collapse."

"Surely there must be something that can be done," Arthur said.

"One could try to play with the cosmic forces directly. But that would be very dangerous."

"How can anything be dangerous when the result otherwise will be the destruction of the universe?"

"The collapse of the universe isn't the worst that could happen to you. You always stand a chance of being okay in the new universe. But it's possible to screw up in this universe in a way that's worse than bad."

"I don't see how."

"You'll note that in all this there's been no talk of hell."

"Are you saying I'll be sent to hell if I don't succeed?" Arthur asked.

"I'm trying to tell you that the usual ideas about hell are wrong. Hell is reserved for those who, like Prometheus, tried to handle cosmic forces and failed."

"What is this hell like?"

"What is pain like? How do you characterize anguish?"

Arthur got the point. But he wondered, "Why would the universe do this? What is this hell? A separate realm? How many realms are there?"

"The universe, the realm of the gods, godspace, hell, the fractal dimension, the realm of avenging dieties, which is where you'd go, and the countless others, are not neat locations. They are spheres of influence that interpenetrate one another. But where you're going, there's no way back."

CHAPTER 56

DEXTER LEFT. ARTHUR THOUGHT ABOUT IT AND DECIDED HE had to do something. He went out to the backyard to say good-bye to Mellicent.

She was worried when she learned where he was going. "But that's worse than death! Didn't anyone warn you?"

As they talked, a new evaluation of Mellicent and himself shaped up in his mind. He saw his going out into the universe as the act of a bold man. He thought, If I'm ready and willing to go out and face the ultimate, whatever that is, am I not willing to say something nice to this goddess whose only fault is that she loves me?

He started to say something to her. And then something unprecedented took place in him. He felt his heart opening to her. He had no words for the waves of emotion that seemed to emanate from his chest and, rising, caused his face to flush. As a result of the forces acting on him now, and his new insight into himself, he was able to take Mellicent into his arms and tell her he loved her.

Mellicent said, "Oh, Arthur. At last."

"Yes," Arthur said. "And now I must go."

"Go? Where are you going?"

"The universe is about to collapse and its all my fault. I must do whatever I can to avert the disaster."

"Don't go," she said.

"I must," he replied.

"Arthur, there is a place we could go to. In this place, the possibilities of experienced time are transformed by love to create an eternity of its own, and this without reference to the passage of time in other places. We could live in a subjective forever, Arthur, and forget all about the universe."

Arthur was tempted to go to this place. He understood what Mellicent was talking about. The importance of love had suddenly become clear to him.

But he also saw that he was not free to go that way. There was a path of duty, a sense of destiny. He knew he had to go forth and try to put matters right.

CHAPTER 57

THE GLOWING GRID LINES WERE ONLY ARTHUR'S FIRST DIS-
covery in this space for which he didn't have a name but
called Godspace for want of a better name. There were other
things in Godspace, quite a few other things, objects with no
doubt special properties. Arthur didn't think he had time to
check them all out, however.

The first thing was to find out what he could do in this
Godspace; because it was becoming apparent to him that his
powers were properties of the space, not of himself personally.
But how was he going to find that out?

Looking around, he saw a great variety of differently
shaped objects. He picked up one experimentally. It was a
soft blue blob, and when he touched it, it grew translucent,
and a voice said, "Welcome to your trip to the beginning of
time. The tour is just about to begin. Keep a tight hold . . . "

Arthur released it at once. It fell with a soft plop. Arthur
shuddered to think how close he had come to a real boo-boo.
That was all he needed, a trip back to the beginning of time.
And meanwhile, what would be happening to Earth?

What he needed was a way to know what all these objects
were and what they did. And he needed to know this before
he fooled around with them and maybe got himself into a lot

of trouble. But how to find out? Was there perhaps some guide that could help him?

Experimentally he said, in a low voice, "Guide?"

Nothing happened.

He said, "What about some help?" And that started something all right.

Lights flashed around him, and a large red cube descended from out of nowhere. On the side of it, in yellow letters, were the words YOUR HELP IN GODSPACE.

"That's a little more like it," Arthur said.

To the HELP box he said, "Hello?"

"Hiya," a voice said in reply.

"Are you indeed the help?"

"I am the HELP file," the voice said. "And you called me up just in time. You really need help to navigate around in this area. I'm surprised they just put you in here without any warning."

"I'm surprised myself," Arthur said. "But it's an emergency situation."

"It's gotta be that," the voice said, "because you've been really foolhardy."

"I just took a couple of steps," Arthur said.

"Yes, but you did it without initiating a step-erasing procedure."

"Is that bad?"

"It's dangerous. There are scavengers in this space who lock onto footsteps."

"Am I in danger now?" Arthur asked.

"Just a minute," the voice said. "I'll check."

In a few moments the voice spoke again. "No, its beginner's luck or something, the scavengers are over in Sector 22CA. You wouldn't believe the mess we've got over there. But that needn't concern you. What seems to be the trouble?"

"Aliens," Arthur said. "I need to do something about them."

"I'm an alien myself," the voice said.

"I'm talking about the ones who are coming to attack Earth."

"Oh, *those* aliens. The *bad* aliens. I was wondering when someone would get around to doing something about that."

"That's what I'm here for."

"But you're not a trained alien killer, are you?"

"As a matter of fact, I'm not."

"That's going to make it more difficult."

"I'm sorry to hear that."

"I'm sorry to have to tell you."

"That's understood. So how should I go about it?"

There was a silence, and then an odd clicking noise. Arthur took that to be the noise the HELP file made when it was thinking. At last the HELP file said, "These aliens? How are they to be delivered to Earth?"

"In a spacefleet," Arthur said.

"A large spacefleet?"

"I presume so," Arthur said. "I believe it would take quite a large spacefleet to successfully attack Earth."

"I would assume so as well," the HELP file said. "And how do you think this fleet will attack? In single file formation, or spread out on a long front?"

"I don't really know," Arthur said. "On a large front, I would imagine. That's the way I'd do it."

"Sounds reasonable to me. I don't suppose you'd have a guess as to the shape this front will take?"

"No idea at all," Arthur said. "But a rough rectangle or crescent would be a likely assumption."

"Oriented what way? Broad-on or end-on?"

"I have no idea," Arthur said.

"Well, we'll assume a worst-case scenario. Let's say they'll be spread out over anywhere from a thousand to a million miles of space."

"That seems reasonable," Arthur said.

"Well, it's obvious to me that in order to cover all possibilities, there's only one defense we can turn to."

"And that is?"

"We need to interpose something between this spacefleet and the Earth."

"Exactly my idea," Arthur said. "What would you suggest?"

"There's only one object I can think of that would do the trick. A black hole."

"What would that do?"

"If we position it correctly, it'll swallow them all up. And that, for all intents and purposes, will be the end of them."

"That's exactly what we want," Arthur said.

"Seems a little hard on the aliens, however."

"They brought it on themselves," Arthur said. "They shouldn't be attacking Earth in the first place."

"You'll get no argument out of me on that," the HELP file said. "I'm Terracentric in my views. So if you agree, that's what we'll do."

"I agree," Arthur said. "What do we do first?"

"Now comes the difficult part," the HELP file said. "First we need to find a black hole of suitable size."

"And then tow it into position?"

"Well, yes, that's the general idea, but we have a number of steps to go through first in order to accomplish that. These are dangerous steps, and any one of them could bring about your obliteration. And mine, too, I might add."

"Oh, dear," Arthur said. "I'm willing to risk it for myself, but I have no right to bring you into it."

"Not to worry about that," the HELP file said. "I'm not concerned with self-preservation. After all, I'm only data. But there's a further difficulty."

"Tell me what it is."

"Well, you see, I usually just sit around rather passively until someone asks me something. Then I look it up and give the answer. No initiative, if you see what I mean. But in this case, I'll need to be more enterprising. More forthcoming. Because you don't know diddly. No insult intended, of course."

"And none taken. I'll need to be more enterprising, too."

"Good. Let me see now. We need to decide what is the correct order in which to take things. I suppose we should find our black hole first."

"That seems correct to me," Arthur said.

"Right. Off we go, then."

CHAPTER 58

WITH ARTHUR IN ENHANCED MODE, THERE WAS NO DIFFI-
culty getting around space, a lot of it, in quite a short time.
The HELP file taught him how to recognize black holes. They
were black, of course, and stood out in sharp contrast to the
pale opalescence of space. Once Arthur knew what to look
for, he saw them everywhere. They seemed to come in all
sizes, from tiny ones the size of blackheads, to gigantic ones
the size of thunderclouds.

"What about that big one over there?" Arthur asked,
pointing inferentially to a black hole the apparent size of a
really big bank of thunderheads.

"Too big," the HELP file said.

"I would think the bigger the better," Arthur said.

"Yes, you might think that, but you'd be wrong. The really
big ones are much less dangerous to an alien spacefleet than
the smaller ones. We have to take into account the inverse
proportion effect here. It's the smaller ones that really do a
job of shredding and tearing."

"Why don't you just pick one out?" Arthur asked.

"I see just what we need," the HELP file said. "See it over
there, to your left? About the size of a two-car garage, rela-
tively speaking. That one's big enough to engulf any space-

fleet on any imaginable front they care to operate on, yet
small enough to do a thorough job of tearing and shredding
them."

"Fine," Arthur said. "Let's get over there and tow it into
position."

He directed himself toward the black hole, but the HELP
file called him back urgently. "You'll get killed if you try to approach it directly. Even in your enhanced mode, it'll make
mincemeat of you unless we do what is needed to handle it
safely."

"What is that?"

"First of all, and before anything else, we need this." He
extruded a device from a handy slot.

"What's that?" Arthur asked.

"A scalar. It's a device that renders any object displayed on
it of moot or indeterminate size. That makes them easier to
handle. By applying the scalar to the black hole, and to ourselves as well, we will be able to move it into position. After a
few more necessary steps, that is."

Scalar in hand, the next step was to enter the dimension without scale, also known as the fractal dimension. This was not
easy for Arthur, although the HELP file told him all he needed
to give up was his preconceptions and change his biased value
judgments to a more even-handed acceptance of "things as
they were."

This was a move that Arthur found difficult, because he
was accustomed to a realm of relativity in which large and small
remained in proportion to each other and never changed.
But the dimension without scale didn't work like that. Here
things were only as large as they needed to be in order to ren-
der the degree of detail required. But they were in themselves
not large or small. The scale of everything compared to everything else could be mapped up or down, since nothing had

an actual or literal size. One thing could be scaled up or down in relation to another thing and so anything could be larger or smaller than anything else without loss of its individual idiosyncracies.

It took Arthur a while to learn this way of thinking, but he had to do it because this was the prerequisite to getting into the fractal dimension.

At last he mastered it, and almost immediately the objects around him became manageable. By scaling the black hole down and himself up, Arthur could move it with his own hands.

"That's fine," the HELP file said. "But now in order that the black hole operates properly, we have to change back to normal size and get some permissions."

But first, it was time for a reconoitter. Arthur, reduced to his human size, now approached the black hole, accompanied by the disembodied voice of the HELP file. As he drew nearer, he saw that the black hole, which had appeared as a solid black object from a distance, closer up had a visible light-colored band around its middle.

As he drew closer, he saw that there were shifting colors and shapes in the band, though he could not make them out distinctly yet.

"What's that band?" he asked the HELP file.

"That's the event horizon," the HELP file said.

"I thought the event horizon was always on the inside of a black hole, made up of light that couldn't get out due to the extreme gravity, or something like that."

"You've got the general idea," the HELP file said. "The true event horizon is of course on the inside. But since nobody can see it there, what good is it?"

"I don't suppose it's much good at all," Arthur said. "But what difference does that make?"

"Quite a lot of difference," the HELP file said. "The singularity that lives in the heart of the black hole is always very proud of his event horizon, and anxious that others look at it, too."

"What does the singularity have to do with it?"

"Just about everything," the HELP file said. "There's no black hole without a singularity, and no singularity permits his black hole to exist without an external event horizon. It is an equivalent to the sexual display certain birds of your planet engage in. There are few sights in the galaxy more beautiful than a full-grown singularity flaunting his event horizon."

"That's not what our scientists think," Arthur said.

"Of course not. But they've never really gotten to know a black hole, have they?"

"I suppose not," Arthur said.

As they draw near, Arthur could see all sorts of events being portrayed on the external event horizon. There were animated pictures of ancient warriors in full armor, there were cities growing out of dense jungle, and priests making sacrifices from high mountain tops.

"How do those pictures get there?" Arthur asked.

"They are beings who have been trapped inside the event horizon."

"But how did they get there?"

"The ancient ones of Earth had many techniques which you moderns know not of. Some of them didn't work so well."

"So it would seem," Arthur said. "And are all those people and things in there still?"

"Virtually," the HELP file said.

"Let's get this thing going," Arthur said.

Arthur moved toward the black hole. It was a shiny smooth black sphere with a bright band. He glanced at the pictures on the band and moved on past it. Now everything ahead of him was dark, and he could feel something tugging at him. He continued moving forward, keeping his balance while something pulled at him.

Then he was on the black hole's surface. It wasn't hard after all; contrary to his expectations, it was soft and he was sinking into it.

And then he was inside the black hole. He looked around. There was a violet light that suffused everything. Something was moving toward him.

Arthur was startled, and considered retreating, but the HELP file said, "It's all right, this is what we came here for. That is one of the black hole swimmers."

Arthur waited while the creature approached. It appeared to be something like a leopard and something like a shark. Its shape didn't stay constant. It was walking toward him, but it also seemed to be swimming toward him.

Arthur waited, and when it got up close it sniffed him.

"Say something to it," the HELP file suggested.

"Good boy," Arthur said. He reached out and patted it on the head.

The creature made a luxurious stretching motion, and an indescribable sound which Arthur interpreted as one of pleasure.

"Now climb on its back," the HELP file said. "Go ahead. It won't bite."

Arthur was none too sure of this but got up on the creature's back. It turned and began loping away. It was running across, but it was also running downward, through the impalpable substance of the black hole.

"How is it able to do this?" Arthur asked the HELP file.

"It is adapted for living here," the HELP file said. "When you are in contact with it, you are able to take on many of its properties."

"How come it's not affected by the properties of the black hole?"

"It is a time-binder," the file explained. "It is using future time, when the black hole will have dissolved."

"How is it able to do that?" Arthur wanted to know.

"It is a very great mystery," the HELP file says. "Only a few creatures are able to draw on future time like that. There's a price, of course. It uses up its own present time in order to access future time. It's borrowing from its own future."

"So what happens to it?"

"When it's used up all its future time, the time debt must be paid."

"How is that done?"

"It disappears."

"Where does it go?"

"We don't know," the HELP file told him. "There's a conjecture that there's a special place that exists where time debts can be paid off by hard manual labor. But that's by no means certain."

Arthur returned his attention to the creature. Riding on its firm yet yielding back, he could feel himself sinking inward. Suddenly the creature stopped, turned, and appeared agitated.

"What's going on?" Arthur asks.

"It must have picked up a parasite," the HELP file said. "Parasites exist in this place, too. They drain the host of present time."

"What is there to do?"

"The time creature can take care of it. As long as there's only one."

Arthur watched as the time creature burrowed into its own flank. Its jaws flashed, and Arthur got a glimpse of white teeth. There was a sort of squeaking sound and the time creature resumed its downward trip.

"It's all right this time," the HELP file said. "But it could have been dangerous if there had been a number of them. The time beast would have had to fight them off or die. You would have been thrown from its back."

"What would have happened then?"

"You would have become a part of the event horizon."

Penetrating to the center of the black hole, they came to the singularity. The singularity was indescribable. This was to be expected, since each singularity was different, one of a kind, in a word, singular.

This one took on describability. It looked at first like a ball of wiry black hair out of which two bright eyes peeked.

"Singularity?" Arthur asked tentatively.

"Yes, I am the singularity. And you are a human, unless I miss my guess."

"No, you're right, I'm a human."

"Well, what can I do for you?"

"I'd like to ask permission to move your black hole."

"Where to?"

"Not very far away. You see, I want to put it in the path of an invading spacefleet."

The singularity rotated slowly while it thought. Each way the singularity turned, it presented a different look. And each time it turned, its look changed again. Many of its appearances were so complex that Arthur couldn't think of anything to liken them to. Some, however, were familiar: a cross-section of a cliff, a green 1938 Oldsmobile, a knife edge with a nick in it, a charming young woman with orange hair, and so on. There seemed no end to the shapes the singularity could assume.

"So how did you like my event horizon?" the singularity asked after it finished its changes.

"It was wonderful," Arthur said.

"Wouldn't you like to become part of it?"

"Not really. I mean, I'm sure it would be nice if conditions were different."

"Perhaps I can make that happen," the singularity said. "I'd really like to add you to my collection."

"Hey, leave the kid alone," the HELP file said. "He's just trying to save his planet."

"Well, what's that to me?" the singularity said. But it didn't ask again.

CHAPTER 59

NO SOONER HAD ARTHUR SUCCEEDED IN GETTING THE BLACK hole into position than he heard a voice.

"Boy, what you doing with that black hole?"

Arthur looked around. A tall, thin, semitransparent entity with a long nose had just showed up.

"Do I know you?" Arthur asked.

"You're about to. I'm the cosmic censor. Now, what were you doing with that black hole?"

"Just moving it over here," Arthur said.

"And who in tarnation told you to do that? Damn it, boy. You're fooling around with forces beyond the petty limits of your feeble imagination. You're going to create a tenth-order paradox and screw everything up. As the ultimate guardian of the universe, I think I should just cut you out of this entire sequence. That's by far the simplest solution."

"I won't permit it," the HELP file said.

"Get out of my way, sonny, or I'll excise you, too."

"You can't do that. I'm a hidden system file."

The censor's voice turned mean. "Listen up, babe, I can excise hidden files just like any other kind. Get out of my way."

The HELP file spread his long wavery arms protectively around Arthur.

"And stop that," the censor said. "You're personifying, trying to make a pathetic human situation out of the boilerplate of universal necessity. Nothing like this is taking place. You're falsifying the data."

"At least I'm making it comprehensible," the HELP file said.

"I'm telling you now for the last time: Get out of my way."

"This is historically unsound," the HELP file said.

"History is of no interest to me," the censor said. "It may be as you say. I don't know and I don't care. What I know is the rules. And the rules forbid this sort of thing."

"But if Earth is destroyed, the rules will vanish, as will you."

"No, the rules are eternal. Even after mankind is long gone, even after the universe has stopped manifesting even as a memory—the rules, the eternal rules will still be there. I am sorry, but I'm going to have to censor Arthur."

He began to do so, grasping Arthur with rubbery fingers that exuded unreality. Arthur grew pale, transparent, began to fade out. And then the HELP file, with an inarticulate cry, leaped forward and interposed himself.

"I won't let you subvert my function in this way! I've promised this man I'd look out for him. Leave him alone!"

"Then it's your ass for breakfast!" The censor roared.

There was a tussle. The HELP file lost, as was to be expected.

The HELP file said, in a faint voice, "He's got me . . . but you're safe. If he excised both of us, it would set up a contradiction he couldn't explain. You're safe from him, for now. I've tried to leave a trace, so the controllers of the universal machine will know what happened. Tell them . . . I tried to help . . . "

The HELP file collapsed and disappeared.

Arthur had triumphed. The black hole was in position.

Arthur watched as the alien fleet steamed into it, while from a different angle Leafie and his cohorts did likewise. They were all obliterated in a cataclysm whose descriptive potential beggared the imagination. Victory at last! But Arthur's triumph was short lived. For now he was snatched away in mid-huzzah by the High Gods, who had been watching and biting one another's fingernails in anticipation.

Arthur was going to have to pay for this big time. It was showdown time.

PART 8

CHAPTER 60

THE PLACE TO WHICH THE HIGH GODS BROUGHT ARTHUR looked like nothing so much as a courtroom back on the planet Earth. It had rows of seats facing a raised podium. In the center of that podium was a large lectern, and sitting behind it were a group of beings whom Arthur recognized as the High Gods.

These god-judges were radiant and terrible, and they gazed sternly at Arthur, who took his place in a little enclosure.

A creature of some sort strode forward. It was a robot, or at least a manlike thing of metal, with a burnished skin that dazzled the eye.

"You are Arthur Fenn?" the robot asked.

"I am," Arthur said.

"Arthur Fenn, you are accused of the highest crime it is possible to charge to a human. That crime is the releasing of forces that upset the balance of the universe and bring to oblivion all who dwell in it, gods, men, creatures of every sort, living and nonliving; yes, all this, and even stars and quarks, even matter, that fundament upon which both existence and being in the phenomenal world is based. Prisoner, how do you plead?"

Arthur opened his mouth preparatory to answering, but just then a being stood up from the audience and said, "Noble judges, may I be permitted to speak for this man?"

The judging gods looked at the being who had spoken, and one of them said, "And just who the hell are you?"

"I am that which speaks for mankind when it cannot speak for itself."

"Oh, you must be the lawyer for the defense," the judge on the right said.

"I have the honor to be that entity," the being said.

"Well then, what do you have to say for the prisoner?"

"Most learned and august judges," the being said, "I who speak here am not truly a living being. I am a personified principle of justice. I just wanted us all to be clear about that. Let me say that this Arthur is a typical man, who knows not where his minor beginnings may lead. Judges, it is not Arthur's fault that he availed himself of all means in his power to overcome the doom that was approaching him on little Earth so lone. Consider, gentlemen, the plight of this man, who, in the simplest terms, made a foolish business venture and stood to go to jail for it. You may think in your wisdom that jail is no big deal and that Arthur had no right to threaten the universe with destruction for his own selfish ends. I would argue that. But even accepting it, I must point out that the plaintiff had no notion of where his actions would lead him, and therefore he is not to be blamed since he was not his own prime mover."

"Now just a moment," the prosecutor said. "Willful destruction of the universe is not the only charge. There's more. When the goddess Mellicent granted him demigod powers, what did he do for her in return? Refused to give her the one thing she most desired. Love, in its essential and earthly form."

"I wanted to," Arthur said. "I just wasn't able."

"Yet we know the wish is father to the deed," the prosecutor said cuttingly. "In this case, your inability masked your reluctance to commit yourself to the only great thing in the world between a man and a woman or a goddess. In fact, judges, inability is the whole story for Dr. Fenn. When it occurred to him to clean up the mess he had made, what did he do? Compounded the problem by conniving with a corrupt HELP file to effect his change through the forbidden fractal dimension. And when the guardian of the public good, the universal censor, attempted to expunge him, what did our Arthur do? He refused, and got the HELP file to protect him, at the cost of its own life."

"Hey, I never asked the HELP file to do anything!"

"Arthur's refusal to yield destroyed the censor, who has never been the same since. And it started the great change which has caused the balance wheel to turn, and you, learned fellow gods and judges, to come to life in order to adjudicate the results."

"You're twisting everything!" Arthur howled.

"I am telling it as it was, without your specious attempts at explaining away your passivity, selfishness, and general ineptness."

A judge cleared his throat. "It's all pretty clear. The statements of the defense seem to me a lot of poppycock. In a generalized and overall sense, no one is to blame for anything. But it is equally true that in a generalized and overall sense, everyone is responsible for everything. Or do you disagree?"

"Not I, Your Honor," the lawyer for the defense said. "I myself am but a generalized lay figure, here for the purpose of saying something in the defendant's favor, lest that other world whose existence we dimly intuit were to feel that this is a kangaroo court being held in the interests of a superceded determinism."

"Well said," the leading judge said. "Your caveat has been noted." He turned to Arthur. "Prisoner, rise and face us."

At that moment Mellicent stood up, her face wan with concern.

"Will the court permit me to speak?"

"Go ahead," the leading judge said grimly.

"Know, my lords, that I am a goddess of love, Mellicent by name. I may not look much like a love goddess at the moment, having had a bad time of it recently, but it is true. Judges, you have not heard all. I repudiated this man when he refused to love me, but it was a sin of pride on my part. After all, I had come to him in my original form, which had been voted 'most fetching' by generations of my worshipers. I thought that would be good enough for him. And when it was not, when he had the temerity to not love me, I went off in a huff. But then I received good advice from several important beings, including the original love goddess, Aphrodite."

Aphrodite, veiled, had been sitting in the back of the court. She stood up and took a bow.

Mellicent continued. "It was Aphrodite who taught me those fateful Latin words I had not known before: *De gustibus no disputandum*. For the children and dumbheads in the audience, that means there's no disputing taste."

There was a reverent silence. Everyone listened as deep mysteries were unfolded. Everyone felt better for having heard some Latin quoted.

"It was not this man's fault that he didn't love me. I had not taken that form which would please him. The fault was mine."

She turned to face Arthur. "Arthur, what do you think of me now?"

And Arthur answered truthfully, "You're the most beautiful thing I've ever seen." And, having learned a modicum of cunning, did not add, "after Mimi."

Applause in the courtroom. But the judges rapped their gavels.

The leading judge said, "Arthur Fenn, we find you guilty of the crime of having put into play forces that could result in the destruction of the universe. We note also that though you are guilty, you are not, in an ultimate sense, responsible. Despite all that, we note that you are directly implicated in the oncoming destruction of the universe, and when it comes there will be a die-off that would have to be seen to be believed, a die-off that will last until, in its own time, the mega-universe reconstitutes this local universe with entirely different creatures and in accord with a new plan."

The leading god raised his hand. There was a flash of light for emphasis.

The judge continued, "There's just no getting around it. This Arthur Fenn is the original source of the disturbance that has bid fair to destroy our universe. Selfishly and without forethought, Arthur did call up the ancient minor gods who were no good the first time around, and a lot worse the second. When these gods contrived to turn Earth to their own devices, he did nothing, even going so far as to accept a role as their prophet."

"I had no choice," Arthur said hotly.

"You could have said no."

"They would have killed me!"

"So?"

He had no answer to that.

After silence had resumed, the leading judge stated the decree.

"The prisoner must make amends to the universe which he has tried to destroy. To do this he must allow us to involve him in a change that will not harm him and which will give the universe a chance to survive."

That sounded pretty good. "What do you want me to do?" Arthur asked.

"Let us turn back the clock," the judge said, "to that time

still fresh in recent memory when you invested your money in the Brazilian gold mine. That was the beginning, the point upon which the future of the universe rested. It was what you did after that that brought on the ill results."

"Look, I'm sorry about that," Arthur said. "But what can I do?"

"You can go back!" the judge thundered.

"What?" Arthur said.

"Back, I say, to that time in which you made your fateful choice; back to the decision that put all else into play. I refer to the moment of your telling your sleazy friend and broker Sammy to invest your money in Amalgamated of Bahia."

"But he advised me!"

"Yes, but you followed it, didn't you? You are responsible for what you did, not Sammy."

"Okay, I'll grant that. What are you getting at?"

"That you go back to that moment."

"How am I supposed to get there?"

"With our help, of course, since you cannot be expected to turn back time all by yourself. We'll help you return to that moment, and so correct the present disastrous course of history."

"Can you really do that? Put me back in time?"

The judge-god smiled and nodded at the other judge-gods. "Hey, if we all put our minds to it, sure, we can do it. I'll grant you it's a paradox, but less of a universe-buster than what you were doing with that black hole."

"If I do that," Arthur said, "won't I go to jail?"

"I think we can arrange a better result than that. We will send you money ourselves. It'll be another minor miracle, but one more won't matter. And you'll be safe and the universe will be safe."

Arthur thought about it. "That means I'll never get to meet Dexter or Scabber."

"Hey, it's too bad, but is it such a great price to pay?"

"And I won't meet Mellicent."

"So you'll meet some other lady."

"But not Mellicent."

"Don't keep us standing here with your quibbles. There are plenty of women out there, and even quite a few goddesses. Since it seems to bother you, we can set something up for you. A date, I believe you would call it. But this is the way it's got to be. What do you say?"

"What's my alternative?" Arthur asked.

"An infinity of pain which we'll stretch to fit how ever much time the universe has left to run."

"You don't leave a guy a lot of choice," Arthur said.

"We don't mean to," the judge replied.

It was in Arthur's mind to agree. But then something turned in him, something he hadn't even known was there. Although he couldn't put a name to it, it was his own fidelity to the way things are.

He said, "No, I won't do it. To hell with you, go do your damndest. I love Mellicent! And I've done nothing wrong! I'll not agree to change anything!"

"But what about the universe?" the judge asked.

Arthur said, "As a matter of fact, I refuse to participate in a universe that comes apart because of something I did."

CHAPTER 61

"WELL, THAT DOES IT," THE JUDGE SAID. HE WAS ABOUT TO SAY something really awesome when suddenly a great tear appeared in the ceiling of the courtroom.

"Not yet!" the judge cried.

The rip widened, and behind it was the matte black of nothingness. The judges tried to get out of the way, but the opening widened and engulfed them in blackness, and then they were gone and it was as though they had never been.

Arthur ran from the witness box, but his action was not to save himself, for he had given up the self-preservation thing, though in an admirable, upright self-choosing way, not in a state of passivity and apathy such as had characterized him before his big change. This Arthur, slightly but significantly modified from the previous Arthur, ran to Mellicent. He held her in his arms.

Even at that moment as the tear widened to engulf him, Arthur was thinking, My, doesn't she smell wonderful!

And then the great brazen head of Francis Bacon, which had been viewing all this from its corner that Arthur hadn't noticed before, opened its brass jaws and cried, "Time is, time was, time has been!"

The universe wavered, disappeared.

The universe reappeared. Subtly changed.

For one thing, the judges weren't.

Everybody else was.

"Am I dreaming or is this really happening?" Arthur said to Mellicent.

"You're dreaming and this is really happening," Mellicent said, tightening her arms around his neck.

And Arthur thought, I may not be a god myself, but still I did what no god was able to do. I saved the universe. Or maybe I destroyed it and created a better universe. Comes to much the same thing.

The future was uncertain in this new world, with this new woman, in this new life. That could be tolerated. He took one step forward, then another.

And then suddenly there was a silence that issued forth more strongly than noise. Blackout. And then the lights came on again.

Arthur found himself alone on a vast stage, peering out into an audience that easily numbered millions. He realized he had been granted unlimited binocular vision. He could cast his gaze back and back along the fleeting rows of seats receding behind other rows of seats, themselves but a partial expression of just how big that audience was. He was alone on that stage, under the brilliance of lights set into the heavens, lights that picked him up from every angle and illuminated him to the ultimate degree.

A voice as big as all outdoors said, "Welcome, Arthur. It is new universe time."

"But what happened to the old universe?"

"It vanished into the forgotten memories of all the past universes that ever were."

"And I suppose I get the blame for this?" Arthur asked.

"Blame? No! You are to be congratulated, rather, because through you the new thing has come into being."

An invisible chorus now took up the chant: Arthur is great!

The universe said, "Now let's have some bows from the principal characters who served the old universe so well. Come out, everybody, and take your bows."

Ahriman and Asturas came out on the stage, bowed, and vanished.

Sammy and Mimi came out. They both waved. And vanished.

Out came Scabber, Dexter, Leafie, Rotte, Luuma, Yah, and a new god, Rauwolfia, who had appeared at the very end and hadn't had time to get onstage. Still, he was allowed to make an appearance, and then vanish.

Mellicent came out, smiled mysteriously, and vanished.

Various other characters came out; people Arthur didn't even remember. They were given their moment and then they, too, vanished.

"Do I vanish now, too?" Arthur asked the voice.

"Oh, no, Arthur," the voice answered. "You were responsible for bringing me into being. You alone of the entire old world will stay, and on you we will build our future."

"Huh?" Arthur asked.

"You're the new standard," the voice of the universe said. "You are the local ruler of everything. And to show our gratitude, we're giving you a brand-new woman to mate with when you get around to it."

There was a light skirl of drums and a beautiful woman appeared on the stage beside Arthur.

"Hi," she said, "I am the female personification of the new universe. I've been selected for you, Arthur. I'm the one who's really right for you."

"Are you sure?" Arthur asked.

"You'll see," she said, winking.

"And now," the voice of the universe said, "I hereby declare that this is Arthur's universe, and everything in it is here to please Arthur, and if not, they'll have me to answer to."

Tremendous applause.

"We've laid on a feast for you," the voice of the universe said. "We thought it as good a way to begin as any."

A long table appeared laden with delicacies.

Arthur said, "You know, this is a little embarrassing, but I'm really not hungry. I had a snack just before all this. I didn't know . . . "

"He has the right, this man," the universe said, "to be not hungry when he so pleases. But he can also choose to be hungry if he would so desire. What say you, Arthur, would you like to be hungry?"

"Yes," Arthur said. "I think that would be nice."

A moment later, he was ravenous.

He sat down at the head of the table. And the lights went out. Then they came back on again.

An offstage voice said, "Welcome to the new universe, Arthur. We're not sure what we're going to do with you. Certainly not the embarrassing stuff the recent new universe had been intending for you."

"What happened to that universe?" Arthur asked.

"It ended," the new universe said.

"So quickly?"

"There's no schedule for how long a universe is supposed to last."

Arthur saw that he was just going to have to wait for the next thing to happen, just like any slob.

And so the new thing had begun, with Arthur playing an important part in it, but without any of the people and gods and goddesses he had known. Without even the female per-

sonification of the universe, who had been his intended. A
new universe, and no one in it to mate with!

Arthur was not too disappointed, however. Somehow he
had been expecting something like this. This was just the sort
of a stunt you'd expect a new universe to pull.